FALSE MANIFESTO

Book 4 of The Thunderstrike Diaries

WENDY METCALFE

CHAPTER ONE

I was nervous as Thunderstrike approached his downjump at Xalvador Station. We needed to get Zana Vatan safely to her ship, but we might meet trouble here. I'm a Predatorbot, and fierce female lions aren't supposed to fret. But I do.

"Downjump in three… two… one…" Strike cut off his com at the last microsecond before emergence, as usual. Strike was the snarky, smart machine intelligence of the Human Collective frigate *Thunderstrike*, and he delighted in showing off his abilities like this.

The view outside changed to black and stars. We were in normal space. But the nav plot Strike received was anything but normal.

"We have a blockade here," he said. "Civilian ships, some not running IDs. Starnavy briefing coming over now." He put the text up on the wallscreen. "So, it's False Manifesto this time. We're going in with *Silverblade* and *Ribbonfire* to help breach the blockade. Our orders are to destroy ships if necessary."

"Oh," Bahar said. She was Strike's captain, a human woman with night-black skin and a cloud of black hair, and a dislike of combat.

Strike turned on his com. "Apologies, Zana, but we'll be delayed a while getting into station. There's a blockade out there by an outfit called False Manifesto, and we have to help break it up before we get into port."

"Blockades are never good," Zana replied. "I hope the *Silver Crescent* is okay." The *Silver Crescent* was the brand new Regulus Lines' freighter that she was about to take command of.

"It's on the other side of station from the trouble," Strike replied. "It should be fine. Microjumping now." On the vid from the rec area I saw Zana buckle her seat restraint. She was an experienced captain. She knew this might get rough.

We emerged between station's bulk and the blockading ships. *Silverblade* and *Ribbonfire* took up positions on either side of Strike.

"Sheilds up. Weapons hot," he said. There was that waver in his voice which always appeared whenever the prospect of killing someone arose. Strike hated doing that. Yes, this Collective Starnavy frigate is a conscientious objector.

My sensitive ears registered the changed hums and whines of his shipbody as his weapons powered up. I was used to that. *Thunderstrike* had been my home for Standards now. The sounds around me were as familiar as the scents Strike put into the blankets in my cat bed.

"Commander's warning them off now," he said, and relayed the broadcast through the control room nodes. "Unidentified civilian ships, this is Starnavy Station Defence Force. We are tasked with dispersing your blockade. Back off and wait for Traffic Control's instructions."

The answer came right away. "We are False Manifesto. We will not do as you order! We are exposing our President's corrupt dealings. If you take orders from a corrupt politician then we will oppose you too."

"Idiots," Bahar muttered. "They're surrounded and outgunned. They can't hope to win a fight. This blockade doesn't make sense."

"It does if the aim was to draw attention to their case," Strike replied. "That little speech was broadcast to every ship in the defence force."

"Who now know False Manifesto exists," I said.

"Yes. And who now know that people suspect the President of wrongdoing," Bahar replied.

"It's clever. Sowing seeds of doubt in the minds of Starnavy troops. They'd never get direct access to so many

any other way," Strike said.

"This is your thirty minute warning," the Commander sent. "If I do not see dispersal of this blockade within that time our ships will commence firing."

"And… the blockade is starting to break up," Strike said.

"That's a relief," Bahar replied.

I watched the nav plot change. The False Manifesto ships weren't docking here. They were making for the jump point.

"Are they jumping from station to station delivering their message?" Bahar asked.

"They'll have to put into port for fuel and supplies somewhere," Strike pointed out. "But for now, they're not our problem. I've just been released from defence duties. Let's get into dock."

The blockade had caused chaos with traffic scheduling, and we had to wait a whole shipboard day before we could dock. Bahar and I did our best to entertain Zana, but we all wanted to get her on station and safely to her new ship as soon as possible.

Eventually Strike docked, and we got ready to go on station. Strike had made contact with Rai, our machine intelligence Unit contact here, who'd confirmed that things were quiet.

Now we had the task of getting a civilian off the military docks. Zana readily agreed to wear fatigues and be invisible. Bahar and I accompanied Zana onto the dock an hour after Second Shift. The dock was just busy enough for us not to stand out, and nobody bothered us on the journey. Nobody bumped into my nose either, which was a bonus.

We were taking Zana to the Regulus Lines offices here, which were on the other side of station's ring, and two levels down from Strike's berth.

The lift lobby was quiet, and we got into a car 2.4 minutes later. It delivered us safely to an equally quiet lobby not far from the Regulus offices. We stepped into the hallway, and I saw a flicker of shadow up above me, in the angle of ceiling and walls.

That's my drones, Strike said over our feed line. *I'm tracking you.*

You might think I'd find the idea of always being observed disturbing, but I've lost count of the number of times Strike's saved us from danger because his drones have been watching over us.

Good, Bahar replied. *We're nearly there anyway.*

We rounded a curve in the ring and the Regulus offices

came into view ahead of us. They weren't as glossy as the other shiplines' buildings on either side of them. Humans can be so stupid sometimes. They'll choose the shiniest-looking ship or line, without ever looking at their safety records. Humans just don't make sense sometimes.

As we approached the building Zana said, "Thanks for bringing me here."

"No problem. Remember to contact Strike if you run into problems."

"You sure you won't mind? I shouldn't be bothering the Starnavy with civilian things."

"We exist so that civilians can safely do their thing," Bahar said. "At least, our bit of it does."

That was a novel way of explaining what the Special Investigations Unit did. What our unofficial Unit really does is act as the Collective's conscience. We've exposed corrupt colony Governors and got them arrested. We've rescued slaves. And we've shut down offshoots of the illegal Predatorbot Programme which produced me. Officially, we'd be classified as traitors if anyone knew about the Unit. But 'traitor' is a nuanced word, as Bahar put it.

Zana's sister Nyla Vatan was my mentor at the Predatorbot Programme. When kill switches were added to our implanted behaviour modules she'd quit, and outed the secret Programme. We strongly suspected that President Jorrak wanted her dead. She'd sensibly gone into hiding, and we didn't currently know where she was. Strike had made it his mission to find Nyla and her four sisters, and to make sure they were safe.

So far, we'd found Fia, Rhian, and now Zana. But that still left Merrill and Nyla out there somewhere.

"Thank you again," Zana said as we reached the entrance to the Regulus offices. "I will keep in touch – with you and with my sisters."

"Good," Bahar replied. "Safe voyaging."

"And to you too." Zana gave us a wave, then walked inside the building.

"Well, that's done," Bahar said. "The third sister found, and as safe as we can make her. I think I've earned the reward of a good lunch."

Bahar and I met Elio and Quindarius at a new café which Elio said had only opened the week before. They were both part of the Unit. Elio was a black-skinned human, and worked as a Loading Supervisor on the commercial docks. Quindarius was an ageing white-skinned human with grey hair and a pointed beard. He favoured brightly-coloured clothes. Today's suit was of brilliant scarlet silk, worn with a deep blue shirt. His boots were the exact same shade of blue.

The three of them ordered lunch, and as they settled in to eat Elio said, "You might like to know that the *Silver Crescent's* loading now. They have a departure slot for First Shift tomorrow."

"So that means all Zana's crew must be aboard. I hope she'll be safe there."

Elio grinned. "You have to let people go sometimes, Bahar. She'll be fine."

Bahar's scent briefly spiked to anger, then she stuffed it down. "True. So what's the news around here?"

"Was rather hoping you could tell us," Elio said. "What was that blockade about?"

"They didn't tell you?"

"Only that it was messing up our schedules."

"Right. It was an outfit called False Manifesto. They were accusing the Starnavy of working for a corrupt President."

"Bet that went down well," Elio said.

"They didn't stick around to find out. They delivered their

message and left."

"That would fit the pattern," Quindarius replied.

"So they've done it before?" Bahar asked.

"Not full blockades, but they have put ships into places which blocked the traffic lanes at Pekado and Kyoko. They did the same thing there. Broadcast their message, and left."

"I can't figure out if they've teamed up with Outlier Action or not," Bahar said.

"I have not found any evidence for that yet."

"That's something, at least."

"We have a Presidential election coming up soon. It will not be long before the candidates start their campaigns," Quindarius said. "My researches indicate that Jorrak will stand for re-election. I think these False Manifesto disturbances are the first shots fired. I suspect we will suffer a lot more unrest before the election takes place."

CHAPTER TWO

As Bahar finished her lunch Strike contacted us over our feed. *I think you should come back to my shipbody now*, he said. *I've been catching up with contacts here, and we might need to make a quickish departure.*

Oh, we're being mysterious, are we? I said.

I'm not. I don't know anything for definite, but station's tense and I don't want us caught up in it.

Fair enough, Bahar said. *We'll start back now.*

"Strike want you back?" Elio asked.

"He does. It's been great to catch up with you again," Bahar said. "Quindarius, if you learn anything important about Outlier Action or False Manifesto, send the files on to Strike, will you?"

"We have already arranged that. I will do that," Quindarius replied.

"Good." Bahar paid for her lunch and stood up. "Come on, Snap. Back to work."

We left the café and made for the lift lobby. We were two levels below Strike's dock, and on the other side of station. It was approaching the start of Third Shift, and the lobby was busy. It took us 6.1 minutes to get into a car, and I'd had my nose bumped twice by then.

The car doors closed on the lobby, and I snarled. Bahar reached down and stroked my neck. "Sorry about that, Snap. It was busier than I expected. I wonder if anything's happening here."

Third Shift was a major leisure period for a lot of station's staff, and would be the key time to cause a disturbance. Don't make trouble where there isn't any, I told myself. Bahar had taught me that phrase. I used it often.

We came out into a packed lift lobby. Bahar stepped in front of me, and I stayed behind her as she forced her way out to the hallway.

That was just as busy. *What's going on here, Strike?* she asked over our feed line.

There are a lot of people gathering in the square ahead of you. Looks like it's a demo or rally of some kind. Yeah, they've just unfurled banners. It's False Manifesto again.

Can we avoid it? Bahar asked.

You can, but you won't like the route.

Meaning?

You'd have to take the Black Halls.

Oh, right. The Black Halls was what Strike called those narrow hallways where what he called 'dodgy trading' went on. It was home to places where people sold illegal drugs, and where humans offered sex for money. That had finally been made illegal throughout the Collective ten Standards ago. And anything the Collective had made illegal was most likely for sale there.

The traders whose shops lined those dingy hallways displayed legal goods in their windows. Strike said the bad stuff was always in a back room, or available on request.

Oh, well, Bahar said. *If we must, we must.*

I'm sending drones to watch you, Strike replied.

Thanks, I said.

I didn't expect any trouble here with Strike's drones watching over us, but Station Security would be fully occupied dealing with the crowds in the square and wouldn't be patrolling here. We were on our own.

We passed a shop displaying silver jewellery. The necklaces had skulls and knives on them. "Why would anyone want to wear a skull necklace?" I asked.

"Because humans are stupid," Bahar replied. "Some men think it makes them look tough."

"How can a piece of jewellery make someone tough?"

"It can't. They're idiots." Bahar thought a lot of men were idiots because they went to incredible lengths to get sex. She described herself as a sex-repulsed aromantic asexual. She didn't do sex.

We passed a bookshop window. "Graphic novels," Bahar muttered. "Very graphic." She hurried me past them, and I saw a shiver run down her back as she strode away from the shop.

We wove our way through a maze of narrow hallways. Bahar strode fast, and her body was tense. Her scent was anxious. We passed only two lone male humans on our way, and each time Bahar's body stiffened-up as they approached.

We turned into a wider hallway. This was the last of the so-called Black Halls, and would take us back out to the respectable part of station. As we approached the junction an unshaven, overweight, human male staggered into the hallway. My nose picked up a whole set of unpleasant scents from him. He stank of stale sweat, and his breath had that sourness which told me he'd drunk far too much of something alcoholic.

That's another thing I don't get about humans. They have the most marvellous senses, and they're capable of such joy, but some of them insist on being miserable, and on chasing joy through the contents of a bottle, or with drugs which damage their bodies. They really are weird.

The man staggered up to Bahar. "Real lifelike petbot you got there, lady. Need to know where you got it, pretty."

Oh, he was one of those creeps, was he? Bahar stepped back from him, and he crowded her personal space again.

Arming drone now, Strike said over our feed. I caught a flicker of darkness in my peripheral vision, and forced myself not to react to it.

"Get. Out. Of. My. Way." Bahar was wearing civvy clothes, but her voice was pure Starnavy command.

"Bitch! Who the hell you think you are? No-one says no to me."

He surged forward and grabbed the front of Bahar's tunic. Bahar raised her arm and chopped down with the side of her hand on his forearm. I heard the crack of breaking bones, and he let go of her with a snarl.

"Bitch!" He swung at her with his good arm. Bahar took the opportunity to slide past him. *Come on, Snap*, she said.

The slob's wild swing unbalanced him. He staggered, then fell over, his head slamming into the wall on the way down.

Bet that hurt, Strike said. *Get out of there.*

We're going. Bahar increased her pace and strode out into the wider hallway. As I followed her, I saw a shiver run down her back.

I had a different worry. That man had been interested in me. Could he know that I was a Predatorbot? Would he blab to someone about me when he came to?

CHAPTER THREE

It took us 37.8 minutes to reach the dock where *Thunderstrike* was berthed. I was tense all that time, half-expecting someone to challenge Bahar and demand to know where she'd bought me, or arrest her for attacking that man.

Station Security have just arrested your drunk, Strike said over our feed. *He's out cold again right now. I think it'll take him a few hours to come round. We should be gone from here by then. I've got a provisional departure slot for half-an-hour's time.*

Bahar broke into a jog. *It's going to take us that long to get back to you,* she said.

Then get a move on.

Oh, right. He was seriously worried about this. Bahar came to the same conclusion, and lengthened her stride. I cantered along beside her. It was good to stretch my spine.

We reached *Thunderstrike's* berth ten minutes before his departure time. The berth information panel showed the departure time flashing, an indication that it still hadn't been confirmed. As Strike opened the lockout gate for us it stopped flashing.

"This is going to be tight," Bahar said, and ran up the

ramp. I trotted up it behind her, and the outer airlock door began to close as I approached the top.

Don't trap my tail, I said to Strike.

I won't, silly. Get in. Strike's tone had that familiar mixture of exasperation and affection to it.

I set my paws on the cold metal of the airlock deck, and 6.7 seconds later the outer airlock door boomed shut behind me. I heard the clicks as the locks fired. The inner door was already open, and I followed Bahar through it into the ship.

Hurry up in the lift, Strike said. *We're on countdown to undock.*

We're coming, Bahar replied.

As soon as I was in the lift car Strike closed its doors and took us up to Deck Two. We walked into the control room as Strike announced, "Five minutes to undock."

Bahar dropped into the captain's seat and I settled into my cleared space beside her. Strike put up the undock checklist for Bahar. It was another of our little rituals. Strike was running everything here, but he'd learned that humans liked to feel they were in control. The checklist showed that he was fully-fuelled, and that he had an official cargo for this run.

"So where are we going?" I asked.

"Zilaya Station. My holds are full of essential tech for Ennor. It was the only way I could avoid getting stuck here at Xalvador. Undock now," he said.

I watched him expertly ease his shipbody away from the berth and turn it around. "Zilaya, here we come," Strike said as the drive came on-line. My sensitive ears registered the change in sound as it fired up, and under my paws the familiar vibrations began.

Our line came up on the nav display, and Strike expertly eased himself onto it. "Zana sent me a file on her way out," he said. "The *Silver Crescent* is bound for Pekado Station. She said they're hauling essential tech for the colony at Iwan. She says the ship's working perfectly."

"And no doubt you talked to Crescent to confirm that." Crescent was the sapient machine intelligence who ran that freighter.

"You know me too well. Anyway, Zana had some interesting news about Boaz Tamoz. The old Regulus CEO had run-ins with False Manifesto at Dracen and Olianna Stations."

"False Manifesto? How does he link to them?"

"Apparently they suspected he'd done some under-the-counter deals with our President. Here's the exciting bit.

Two Standards ago False Manifesto tried to kidnap Boaz at Olianna."

"Oh," Bahar said. Strike hadn't lost his ability to surprise people. His storytelling skills were well-honed that way.

"They didn't succeed in getting him, of course, but they did get lots of exposure for their cause."

"Like the blockade."

"Yes. It seems to be their M.O."

"I wonder if Zana suspected Boaz was a crook," I said.

"Maybe. But the threat of rape was her primary reason for bailing out. She didn't feel safe there," Bahar said.

Even though I'm female, I can't imagine how hard life is for some human women. The Collective has laws which say that every woman has sole control over her body, and what she does with it. But there are still sex slaves. We'd broken up one of those rings four Standards ago. That's the angriest I've ever seen Bahar.

"It makes me wonder if Regulus have preferential routes in the Outliers," Strike said.

"You mean Boaz bribed his way to dominance there?"

"Yes. Which worked just fine while the Outlier colonies were thriving. But if they're not doing so well now it's an expensive way to limit your expansion."

"Especially if the President who granted those favours is shortly going to lose his power," Bahar said.

"We don't know that. We're supposed to be impartial Starnavy, Bahar."

"Says the founder of the Special Investigations Unit."

"Yes, well… Anyway," Strike turned the conversation away from politics. "I learned something interesting from a Judiciary contact. He said Regulus's operating licence is under review."

"That's not good," Bahar replied. "How big is the risk they'll lose it?"

"Before Boaz left I think there was a strong possibility."

"And we just sent Zana off on a Regulus ship."

"Regulus has a new CEO," Strike pointed out. "Things are already changing there. And Zana's aboard a brand-new ship which meets all current safety specs. She'll be safe for a while. Don't fret about her. Oh, I've just been ordered to reduce speed. Some unidentified ships just downjumped. And they aren't running IDs."

CHAPTER FOUR

"They're civilian ships," Strike said, "and I'm picking up a distress broadcast from one of them. It's very feint. Boosting, and sending on to Traffic Control."

"So what happened?" Bahar asked.

"Give me a moment to find out. Oh, looks like they're a False Manifesto mob. They came in from Pekado. They got shot at on the way out."

Bahar's scent spiked to fear. "Zana's on her way there."

"They'll have it under control by the time she gets there," Strike said. His voice wasn't entirely calm. "Some of this mob's systems failed on downjump."

Bahar shivered. "They were damned lucky to come out at all."

"Two of them didn't."

That shocked us into silence. Yes, we knew space was dangerous, it was always a thought 'in the back of my mind' as Bahar put it, but we didn't let it bother us generally. Until a day like this, when somebody didn't come out, and reminded us of the risks we ran.

"I've been ordered to change course. Some of the survivors have lost helm control. Turning off line now.

And… I've been ordered to go inertial on my new heading."

"Don't like being a sitting duck," Bahar muttered.

She'd had to explain that one to me. Humans used sayings which referenced the natural world, but most of them still didn't respect their environments enough.

"I don't either," Strike replied. "Shields going up now."

I heard the subtle change in the sounds around me; the building whine, then the dampening of some of the noises which were so familiar to me. We coasted for a shipboard day. The nav plot showed a cleared area of space where normally lines of ships would be coming and going. Over the hours, tugs and Station Security ships came out to help the False Manifesto group. There were also a scattering of Starnavy ships keeping watch.

Bahar and I were just thinking of going to sleep when Strike said, "Alert. We're being approached by a ship with a Station Security ID."

"Meaning?" Bahar asked.

"It's not on the database. It's a false ID."

"Why do that?" I asked.

"Because… it's trying to scan me. Jamming signals."

"They're sending out a behaviour module access signal," I said.

When he removed my behaviour module Strike had written some code for me to recognize probes for it. He said I might need to know when someone thought I was a Predatorbot. Someone on that ship was looking for one now.

Don't panic, Snap, I told myself. They can't know you're here. It's just a general probe. The access request stopped. "They've gone away," I said.

"Good. Scans on me haven't stopped," Strike replied. "Glad I got that new scrambler update installed recently. Let's warn 'em off."

He routed an audio version of his message through the control room nodes. "Approaching Station Security ship, you are in breach of Starnavy Standing Order 10-I-22. Back off and maintain legal distance." The scan attempts continued. "Arming weapons now," Strike announced. "I won't hesitate to use them. I repeat: back off."

The ship maintained its position. On the weapons console I saw red lights flick up.

"Are you going to shoot them?" Bahar asked.

"I'm going to shoot out their coms arrays," Strike replied. Through the viewport I saw three flares of flame blossom on the ship's hull. "Now they're moving. Stupid idea to call a Starnavy frigate's bluff."

I agreed. Strike didn't like to kill, but he would if necessary.

The ship finally backed off, and I saw two Station Security gunboats close with it. "They're going to arrest our hostile," Strike said. "Just got a Station Security notification that the ship's not one of theirs. They're hauling it in to interrogate the crew."

"That doesn't get us into jump any faster," Bahar said.

"This will, though," Strike replied. "I've got clearance to go to max line speed. Firing up engines now."

The vibrations and whines around me changed again. I studied the nav plot. We were back on our line and making good speed towards the jump point.

"Let's hope nobody wants a report from us," Bahar said.

"I think Traffic Control would object to us being delayed here. They've got enough hassle. I've sent a basic written report in," Strike said. "Hopefully, that'll allow us to slide under the radar."

We went into jump 20.2 hours later. Bahar and I had tried to sleep while we made our way out to the jump point, but our rest had been disturbed.

As soon as we were safely into hyperspace Strike said,

"Go get some proper sleep this time, you two."

Bahar yawned. "Great idea." She stood up.

I scrambled to my paws and stretched out my neck. "I'm going too," I said.

"Then off you go, sleepyheads," Strike said, and opened the control room door for us. "It's a good job I don't need to sleep."

"We wouldn't be doing this if you did," I replied. "We couldn't travel the universe without machine intelligences."

"Agreed. Night, Snap," Bahar said, and disappeared into her quarters.

I walked into mine, and Strike said "It's not night, it's early morning."

I settled into my bed and curled up on my side. "Does it matter? Shipboard time's weird anyway."

True. I'm worried about that scan back there. Strike switched to our private feed line.

I knew you would be. So what do you know about that ship? I asked.

It's an old Starnavy hull. It was decommissioned thirty Standards ago.

So? Station Security often buys old Starnavy ships.

Yes, but remember Zilaya Station said it isn't one of

theirs.   I've been digging around, and its' ID isn't on anyone's database. It's a rogue.

They didn't manage to scan us, so what's the problem?

The problem is that the Starnavy won't leave this alone. Somebody will want to talk to us about why we were the target.

And you're worried they might uncover the Unit?

Well, it's a possibility. Strike sounded prickly.

I wasn't mocking you, I said.   If we're expecting an interrogation, then we need to get our story straight. But there's time to do that tomorrow. Can I sleep now?

By the time we approached emergence at Zilaya Station Strike and Bahar had gone back through his logs for the last five Standards. They'd made sure that we had a plausible story for each suspect incident. This was part of what Bahar called 'walking the tightrope'. We had to look enough like Starnavy to pass as loyal soldiers.

"Downjump in ten minutes," Strike warned.

Bahar and I were in the galley, finishing off our meals. Bahar drained her third cup of coffee, and stood up. "Come on, Snap. Let's see what we face out there."

I followed her along the hallway and Strike let us into the

control room. I settled into my cleared space beside Bahar's seat. Strike counted us down to emergence, and I felt the familiar pressure wave ripple down my flanks. The roiling greys and reds in the viewport changed to serene black and stars.

"I've got our docking assignment. Everything looks normal," Strike said as the nav plot came up on the screens.

"So far, so good," Bahar replied. "Let's hope it stays that way."

Two hours before we docked Strike fed me in my room, and scolded me for being a messy cat, as usual. That was a reassuring sign. It meant things hadn't gone 'pear-shaped', as Bahar put it. Yet.

Strike let me into the control room. Bahar was already there, and she was wearing a Starnavy uniform. Was Strike expecting trouble here? Usually Bahar just wore faded fatigues if we weren't going to be 'on show', as she put it.

Nobody approached us on the way to our berth, and Strike connected to the dock right on schedule. As usual, he started refuelling first. He always wanted to be ready to run.

I sometimes wondered what it would feel like not to be running and hiding all the time. But while the President who'd authorised the Predatorbot Programme still held power, being discovered wasn't an option for me. It would be the quickest way to getting a new behaviour module implanted, and losing my freedom.

"Getting a download from Helsa," Strike said. Helsa was part of the Unit, and she worked in Zilaya Station Security. "Trouble." His voice had gone sharp. "You're ordered to report to the local Commander on station, Bahar. The Starnavy is worried about that scan attempt on us."

CHAPTER FIVE

Bahar went onto Zilaya Station an hour after the start of First Shift, when the dock was quiet. As soon as she'd left the loaders arrived to deliver Strike's cargo for Ennor. He locked me in the control room and sent his drones down to help them. They were stashing the goods into the Xenophon shuttle's holds. Luckily, the cargo was all small boxes of equipment, and it fitted easily.

Strike had sent his drones to watch over Bahar, of course. She reached the briefing room safely, and gave the Commander a brisk salute as she walked in. Commander Mirrek was a white-skinned man with a narrow face which looked too thin. The look wasn't helped by him being bald.

"Sit down, Captain. We're being joined by Station Security this morning." As he spoke, the door opened, and a copper-haired human woman walked in. "This is Ms. Eitan, Station Security Liaison."

The woman gave the Commander a brisk nod, then sat down opposite Bahar. That was odd. The two humans' bodies were stiff. Was there some kind of conflict going on here?

"I've received Strike's files on the scan incident at Xalvador," Mirrek said, "and I need to know why

Thunderstrike is the repeated target of these scan attempts."

"I don't know, Sir," Bahar replied, "but I can make some guesses. We've been asked to do a lot of cargo runs lately, most of them carrying essential tech for colonies. We have noticed there does seem to be more interest in us when we're carrying loads bound for the Outliers."

"Oh, clever, Bahar," Strike said to me. "Let's see how he plays this one."

"Are you suggesting someone wants to interfere with those shipments?"

"Raiders are an ever-present threat. Although they shouldn't know what we're carrying, of course. There is another possibility. I hesitate to mention this, but there are scurrilous rumours going around that President Jorrak has decided the Outliers should be abandoned. I don't believe them, but if others do, that could explain the scans on Starnavy ships known to carry cargoes."

"I'm sure no-one believes those rumours." So, the Commander wasn't willing to consider the possibility of a rogue President.

"It might not be a Starnavy problem, Sir," Bahar said. "When we're carrying supplies for colonies there are civilian contacts on either side of the operation. They have their own sets of records. It's far more likely rogues have got hold of their records than ours. And that might lead them to *Thunderstrike*. Maybe they think they can do a quick snatch of valuable equipment and sell it on the black market."

"I hadn't considered that." The Commander's body relaxed.

Eitan's stiffened further. Clearly, she thought Bahar was criticising Station Security. "We haven't been notified of any data breaches," she said. "Civilian cargoes aren't our responsibility anyway – beyond providing safe spaces to load, unload, and store them."

There was a prickly silence for a moment, then the Commander said, "So you don't know of any other reason why *Thunderstrike* is being scanned, Captain?"

"No, sir. Do you know anything we should be aware of?" Bahar asked.

"Nothing definite. But remember that we have a Presidential election coming up in a Standard's time. We must appear to be above board in all our dealings now. We will be under extra scrutiny from all candidates."

"I'll bear that in mind, Sir."

"Good. Dismissed."

Bahar saluted and stood up. Eitan scrambled to join her.

She had no intention of remaining alone with the Commander.

"What do you make of that, Snap?" Strike asked me as Bahar left the room.

"I thought he was going to talk about the Unit at one point."

"Yes, me too. Well done to Bahar for raising the corrupt President rumours. We're going to have to be extra careful with our Unit contacts until the election's over."

Bahar returned to us 2.3 hours later. She'd decided to do some shopping while she was on station. Strike fretted about the deliveries, even though she'd sent him a list of the stuff she'd bought. He insisted on scanning every container for bugs.

He didn't find any, of course. It was just innocent shopping, but I knew the Commander's briefing with Bahar had worried him. *Thunderstrike* had got onto somebody's radar, and that wasn't good.

He closed the airlock door behind her and said, "All your deliveries have arrived."

"Good. I need coffee. That meeting was too close for comfort."

So she thought so too. Strike brought her up in the lift and she went to the galley. "Go talk to her, Snap," Strike said, and let me out of the control room.

Bahar had already settled at the galley table with her mug of coffee when I walked in. "Hello, Snap," she said. "I'm glad to be back here."

"Glad you got out of the Commander's trap," Strike said.

"What do you mean?" she demanded.

"I think he was testing your loyalty to the President," Strike said. "I've been digging into his records. Commander Mirrek has donated to Jorrak's re-election fund recently. Stupidly, he did it under his real name."

"That's illegal for Starnavy personnel," Bahar said. "Hypocrite! Reminding me that we need to be above board while supporting Jorrak's campaign. It explains his reaction to my allegation, though."

"Indeed it does. He will be reported," Strike replied. His voice had that hint of steel to it that always made me want to shiver. I sure wouldn't like to be on the wrong side of Strike.

He wouldn't do the reporting direct, of course. That was a job for a Unit informant.

"Hopefully that will get the Commander off our trail," I said.

"Hopefully. I've got a provisional departure slot for Ennor in two hours' time… and confirming now. Let's get out of here before that Commander thinks of something else to ask you."

We undocked on the mark, and made our way out to the jump point along a quiet line. As we were about to commit to jump Strike received a priority message from Helsa. "Hope this isn't trouble," he said as he unpacked the encryption. "Oh."

"What?" Bahar demanded.

Strike put a video file up on the wallscreen. "This is Ennor," he said. It's a record of a False Manifesto demonstration there a week ago."

"So why are we interested in this?" Bahar asked.

"Because of this." One of the drones zoomed in on a cluster of figures close to the flapping banners, and I gasped. I recognized that face. It had been stored in my memories for Standards. "She's dyed her hair, but my facial recognition analysis is 99% certain that is Merrill Vatan," Strike said.

CHAPTER SIX

"So what's Merrill doing at a False Manifesto rally? She's supposed to be a neuroscientist," Bahar said.

"It's not too far from neuroscience to psychology. If Merrill studied the psychology of politics, she'd be really useful to that outfit," Strike said.

"Mmm," Bahar replied. Clearly, she didn't like that idea.

"False Manifesto aren't an illegal organisation."

"Yet."

"If they become one, it's far more likely it'll be through the dodgy dealings of our President," Strike said.

"I still don't like the idea of her being tied up with them."

"You can't control people's lives, Bahar."

"I know." She sighed. "We've been at this quest so long; I think I've lost sight of the fact that the Vatans are ordinary humans. Maybe I needed this reminder."

"Anyway," Strike said, "we're on our way to Ennor. Maybe we'll be able to work out what she's doing when we arrive there. I've just received a briefing from Commander Mirrek. I'll just store it and look at it when we're in jump. Time to jump ten minutes."

Once we were safely in jump Strike unpacked the Commander's briefing. "Oh, right," he said.

He put the file up on the wallscreen. Starnavy Intelligence suspected that False Manifesto had a data hub on Ennor. "It's a good location for serving both the Outliers and the Central Worlds," Strike said. "Not too close to Earth to be noticed, but able to get data out both ways. And… here's an order personally signed by our President to destroy any of their data hubs we find."

"Destroy the installations of a legal organisation?" Bahar's voice was full of outrage. "That's not what the Starnavy exists to do."

"The Commander's added a note to the order," Strike replied.

The text came up on the wallscreen. <I am ordered to forward the attached. This is not top priority> it read.

"He's not happy about this," Bahar said. "Which is surprising, given that he's donated to Jorrak's re-election fund."

"Maybe this has made him change his mind," I replied.

"We can hope. I take it we won't be looking for data hubs?" Bahar asked.

"Only if Merrill turns up in one," Strike replied. "It

occurs to me that our President might take matters into his own hands and order his personal troops to search the planet. I've decided to wake up all our people. If Merrill is down there still, we might need them."

Strike carried twenty troops, who spent their time between missions in suspension in Strike's cryo bay. If Strike had decided to wake them up, it meant that he expected trouble on Ennor – and that Merrill was in danger.

We downjumped 5.3 hours later. As soon as we emerged Strike started scanning Ennor's systems. "The usual level of security and coms arrays," he said. "A healthy amount of civilian data traffic."

That meant Strike had hacked into their feeds. He could've made a fortune selling on confidential information. Luckily for everyone, Strike had no desire to do that.

"Credits aren't real wealth," he'd said once when Bahar asked him about it. "Real wealth is knowledge and creativity. Real wealth is using your talents and producing something new, something which didn't exist before you put the words on the page, the brushstrokes onto paper, or set the blueprint down."

I think Strike was jealous of human creativity. He'd never

developed a creative talent of his own, although many sapient machine intelligences had.

Sapient machine intelligence authors had had a long fight to obtain copyright protection for their original works. The early AIs re-used human creativity, stole their work and re-arranged it. But over the last century sapient machine intelligences had grown to be truly creative in their own right. And twenty Standards ago they'd won legal copyright protection for their original works.

"No indication of any trouble down there," Strike said. That meant he'd hacked planetary security's supposedly secure lines. It really was a good thing Strike had such a strong functioning moral compass.

"What about Merrill?" Bahar asked.

"She seems to have disappeared. I can't find any trace of her. Hopefully you'll catch up with her when you drop."

~~~~~

We went into orbit around Ennor 40.2 hours later. Strike woke me from a deep sleep, fed me, and scolded me more than usual when my still-sleepy body made a big mess of my meal. Well, what did he expect? He should've woken me earlier. And not printed the gristly bits.

I left him cleaning up the remains and went to the rec area.
~~~~~

Bahar was there, along with all twenty of our troops. Howin and Rance looked annoyingly alert, but that's what they were paid for. They are our two team leaders. I'm just a lazy lion.

"I've been stripping security bulletins," Strike said. "There's a gang of local toughs who've been impersonating colony officials and stealing their supplies. Leaders are a couple of criminals convicted of theft and violence on several Central Worlds. Sending their mugshots to your implants."

The thugs were both middle-aged white-skinned humans. One had long white hair, scraped into an untidy plait. The other had a deeply-tanned face and short-cropped black hair.

"Received," Howin said. "We'll look out for 'em. So what's our schedule?"

"You're dropping at the shuttleport, on the outskirts of the capital Kavitta. Reps of the planetary government will meet you there to unload your cargo."

"ID?" Rance asked.

"I've told them we'll only hand over the goods to people with this ID." Strike flashed a card up on the wallscreen.

"Easy to fake," Howin said.

"Study the hologram, and engage UV filters. This is what you'll see if the ID is genuine." The image on the screen changed. A name came out of the hologram design. "Only a few key senior security people know this feature exists. Most people don't."

"Okay. So we're wearing armour?"

"You are." Strike briefed the troops about Merrill. "That's your secondary mission. Find her, then I'll send Bahar in to talk to her."

"Right," Howin said. "So we hang around in town and pick up intel when we're done with the cargo?"

"You got it. And you'd better get down to the shuttle now," Strike replied. "You're landing at 09.00 local time."

"On our way," Howin said, and stood up.

I let the troops get settled in the shuttle first before Bahar and I went down to take our places in its control room. I didn't want to be kicked by the troops' boots. They'd done that before, and it hurts. I wore my armour, but it was retracted. This time I'd kept its design a neutral silver colour, with a small bogus petbot logo.

"Seal-up now," Strike said. "And out you go."

The first time I'd done a shuttle drop I'd panicked when *Thunderstrike's* bay doors opened onto black space. I'd absorbed Strike's lectures about the dangers of space too well. Now I still knew it would kill me if things went wrong.. But I also knew that Strike would do his very best to see that nothing did go wrong.

Ennor came into view below us. We'd dropped over the planet's nightside, and the major coastal settlements showed lights. A scatter of lights inland showed the locations of the agricultural hubs.

The terminator came up, and we crossed into the dayside. Immediately, Ennor Traffic Control contacted us, assigning a landing line. Our descent was easy, and the shuttle lowered onto the pad at Kavitta Spaceport 18.7 minutes later.

"Two armoured skimmers coming your way," Strike said. "Not what I'd expect. I'm checking with planetary admin now. They're not their people. You got yourselves some rogues."

"We're out first," Howin replied. "You two stay put." She meant Bahar and me.

"Will do," Bahar replied.

Strike sent us the feed from the shuttle's exterior sensors. The two skimmers pulled up close to the hold airlock. So, they were expecting to take our goods, were they?

"Admin confirms those two skimmers are unauthorised," Strike said.

"Right. Everybody out," Howin ordered. The troops had

sealed their helmets. They looked intimidating in their full armour.

As they appeared outside the shuttle figures got out of the skimmer. *They're carrying pistols. Nothing than can damage your armour,* Strike said. The leader of the approaching group was the white-haired thug from our mugshots. He was dressed in an ill-fitting uniform which had an official-looking logo on it. *Logo on his uniform is planetary cargo handling. I'd guess he stole it.*

And killed somebody to get it, Howin replied.

The view changed. Strike had sent drones out, and now we were getting their feeds. *Definitely our thug,* Strike said. *Just done a face recognition match. Let's see what they want.*

White-hair strode up to Howin. "You have cargo for us," he said.

"I need to see your ID," Howin replied.

That bothered him. He fumbled in his jacket pocket and drew it out. He thrust it into Howin's face.

False, Strike said over the feed.

Howin studied it for a moment, then said, "This is a forgery. You aren't Dagen Kassan, and you're about to be arrested."

"Bitch!" he snarled, and shot at her. Her armour repelled the shot easily.

Stun him? she asked over our feed.

Honestly, how could she keep so calm? Six of the thugs were firing at the squad now.

Planetary Security are approaching now, Strike said. The view from the drones changed, and I saw armoured skimmers hurtling towards the troops. *Those are genuine*, Strike said.

The thugs noticed them too, and our crook turned and ran for his skimmer. *Locking him out*, Strike said, and closed the skimmer's door. The thug almost ran into it, then swore a string of colourful curses.

The rest of the thugs ran right into the approaching Planetary Security troops, who efficiently arrested them and hustled them into their skimmers. They grabbed the white-haired thug after a brief struggle, and hauled him aboard too.

"Well, that's that," Strike said. "And... legitimate Planetary Logistics loader coming out to you now."

Howin insisted on checking their IDs too, but they were genuine, and she supervised the unloading of our cargo. She got the official sign-offs, and the loader left.

So we go into town now? she asked.

New plan, Strike said. *Just got some information that changes things. Come inside for a briefing.*

CHAPTER SEVEN

The troops returned to the shuttle's passenger compartment for Strike's briefing. When they'd all settled Bahar joined them. I stood in the doorway of the control room to listen to the discussion.

"First off, our cargo is now in secure storage. I've sent copies of the signed handover documents to Central Admin. It helps to have that on record," Strike said.

"So you can prove you're doing something legal some of the time," Howin said.

"Exactly. But the reason I got you together now was this."

A garbled transmission came from the nodes. "This was outbound for the ansible."

"Not much use like that," Rance replied.

"It's a novel way of scrambling the signal. Took me all of 2.4 minutes to crack it."

Howin laughed. "What took you so long?"

"Anyway," Strike said, "This is the cleaned-up signal."

"Bulletin from Outlier Action. Arjun has been denied replacement parts for water filtration plants. Naretha has had requests for replacement coms arrays refused. Frizinn…"

Strike muted the feed. "The broadcast is a long list of actions which support the idea that the Outliers are being abandoned. The local ansible routed it to Ataret Station."

"On the Central Spine. Bet it's goin' to Central," Rance said.

"That's my analysis. The important thing from our point of view is that this signal originated from Ennor. And it came from this continent. Location is somewhere here."

Strike put up a map of the continent on the wallscreen. "The transmission keeps moving around. They must be using portable coms arrays. I think the location is somewhere here." He surrounded an area of mountain peaks with a red circle. "There's a whole cave system there."

Howin sighed. "Couldn't be somewhere easily accessible, could it?" she grumbled.

"That'd be too easy for people to discover," Strike replied. "They might be operating under Planetary Security's radar. Provided they're not inciting rebellion Security might've made the decision to ignore them. They are broadcasting truth, after all."

"I take it you think Merrill might be there?" Bahar asked.

"If she's still on planet, then yes. And even if she isn't, those Outlier Action people might know where she's gone."

"If they'll tell us," Bahar replied.

"One problem at a time. Our first objective is to explore those caves, and make contact with people if they're still there."

"Starnavy won't like that," Howin said.

"The organisation isn't illegal. It's our President who'd object to them, not the Starnavy. And if they've been broadcasting those bulletins from here for a while, they might well have attracted Jorrak's attention. Your secondary role is to review their security and advise if necessary."

"Now you're getting morally grey," Bahar said.

"Advising citizens of the Collective on their safety? That's part of the Starnavy's remit."

"Hadn't seen it like that," Rance said.

"You're leaving now," Strike replied. "Traffic Control wants you off the pad. It's getting to peak arrivals time there. Lifting now. You're bound for the mountains."

If Traffic Control had asked Strike for our destination, he'd planned on saying we were going to Carradino. Bahar said it was a resort town in the foothills on the southern side of the Zared Mountains. Apparently, people went riding and shot things there in summer, and in winter they did something called skiing. I had no idea what that was, and I didn't need to know.

Strike said the season there was early autumn, and Carradino should be quiet 'between the summer and winter crowds' as he put it.

We didn't go to Carradino, of course. We did go to the southern flank of the mountains. As soon as we were far enough away from Kavitta to drop off Traffic Control's scans Strike settled the shuttle into a gully. "Time for a drone survey," he said. "Sending them out now."

In the hours until sunset Strike's drones explored the area. He split them into two squads and engaged their stealthing. He sent one squad over the ridge to scan the northern side of the mountains. The second squad searched the southern side. By dusk they'd discovered the openings to eight caves on both sides of the mountains. There'd been no more transmissions, so Strike hadn't been able to find any facility there by riding on their coms signals.

"It's possible those caves interconnect," he said. "I'll send the drones in in the morning."

Everybody woke at dawn. The shuttle was cramped, and not the most comfortable place to sleep. Most of the troops had taken their bedrolls into the vehicle bay and bedded down in between the skimmers. Howin and Rance slept on the floor of the passenger compartment.

Bahar spent the night in the captain's seat, which wasn't as uncomfortable as it sounds. I opted to sleep beside her on the deck.

Strike said I hissed and snarled when I slept. You might think that was a curious thing for a sapient machine intelligence to take an interest in, but Strike was constantly studying us. It wasn't the cold study of some project like the Predatorbot Programme. His study came from pure curiosity. Strike wanted to know everything about the people who lived in his shipbody. That was his way of showing he cared for us.

While we ate Strike sent his drones inside the caves. The three westernmost accesses on both sides of the mountains didn't lead anywhere useful. Two were single caves, the others had narrow passages which were too small for humans to squeeze through. Even the tiny drones had to go slowly along one of them to avoid getting damaged.

"So we know they're not at the western end of the mountains," Strike said. "My guess is the eastern side caves are the same. Let's check."

He sent the drones off again. The two easternmost caves

had no passages in them, but the caves in the central section of the mountains were larger.

The images on the wallscreen showed the drones flying down a passageway which opened-out into a largish cave. "No gear here," Strike said.

"Where are the people?" Bahar asked.

"Good question. Let's see if we can find out."

Strike sent the drones off again to continue their exploration. Passageways radiated out in four directions from the central cave. The eastern passage ended in another large cave, which was also empty. The northern and western passageways led to small caves. The southern one was a dead end.

"Think you need to do an eyes-on examination of that complex," Strike said. "You find things the drones miss."

"Knew you'd say that," Howin replied. "Okay, people. Go get your gear together. Let's get this ascent started."

Bahar and I stayed in the shuttle. Strike sent the drones flying along the southern side of the mountains to provide cover for the squad, and vid for us. He left the drones on the northern side of the mountain in position there. "Best to keep a lookout on both sides," he said.

Howin and the squad spent the day making a steady ascent of the southern flank. The caves were high up on the mountainside, and the troops seemed to make slow progress on their hike. They were wearing their armour, and Strike had them engage the active stealthing. That told me he was worried about surveillance.

At one point they disturbed some sure-footed grazers. The animals went bounding away down the steep slope below them. "Some kind of mountain goat," Bahar said. "I'll never know how they don't break their necks travelling like that."

"Evolutionary adaptation," Strike said.

"Very funny. Are the troops going to reach the top caves before nightfall?"

"No. It's a much steeper ascent than it looks. They'll only get half-way up today. There's a cave they can sleep in part-way up the slope." He highlighted the location on the wallscreen image with a red circle. "They can put up a force shield to keep out any fierce beasties."

"Like my mountain cousins," I said. I'd seen a snow lion creeping along below the squad at one point. Its fur was much thicker than mine, and it was white.

"Indeed. Sending them the location now, and sending a

drone into that cave to check it's safe."

The drone's feed showed that the cave was just one space, and it opened-out beyond the entrance. "Empty. Space to sleep out of the wind there," Strike said. "No roosting things to drop on them. I guess it's too cold for 'em up there." He sent the images and co-ordinates on to Howin.

Good idea, Howin replied. *Light's going. We ought to be heading for shelter.*

It took the squad another hour to reach that cave, and by the time they did it was nearly dark. As they disappeared beyond the entrance Strike said, "That's them settled. Still no sign of any activity up at the target caves. You might as well go sleep too."

I woke at dawn, and Strike fed me. I needed to stretch my back, so he let me out of the shuttle to pace about. I walked to the head of the gully and looked out over the land. An expanse of rough grey rock sloped down to a dense stand of trees below me. They were the ones Bahar called 'coniferous'. Lower down, I could just see the tops of the other types of tree, the ones she called 'deciduous'. Humans and their labels. They always have to complicate things. They're just trees to me.

The morning was fine, and Ennor's star warm on my fur. Strike said it was a 'main sequence yellow star'. I didn't need to know that either.

Bahar came to join me. " A truly unspoiled continent," she said. "I wonder how long it'll stay that way. I guess that depends a lot on who gets elected President in a Standard's time."

We stood for a while, not speaking. The morning breeze was cool, and carried scents of unfamiliar flowers to my nose. Above us a large dark bird soared, dived, then climbed again. It opened its wings and circled higher. It must've found one of those things Strike called 'thermals'.

"Tawny eagle," Bahar said, breaking the silence. "A raptor on the hunt for its morning meal."

I wondered what it would feel like to soar over the land on wings. I could've asked Strike to show me a sim, but it wouldn't be the same. Anyway, I'd never fly. My lion body was too heavy to take off. I had solid bones, and Strike said birds' bones were hollow.

Strike broke our reflection. *Squad's on the move*, he said over our feed.

We'd better go see what they find. Bahar turned and led the way back to the shuttle. *Let's hope we learn something useful today.*

CHAPTER EIGHT

Howin and the troops were up early too, and by the time Bahar and I returned to the shuttle they were finishing their breakfast.

Briefing, Strike said over the feed. *I've sent my drones up to the topmost caves, and I still can't find any trace of the False Manifesto people there.*

So they've moved on, Howin said.

You still want us to go up there? Rance asked.

Hold your position for now. A Starnavy shuttle's just dropped into atmosphere over the nightside. They've made no coms contact with anyone on-planet. Traffic Control doesn't have them in their lines.

Which is suspect, Bahar said.

Indeed. Projected descent path ends at the foot of the northern flank of the mountains. My guess is they're coming to investigate the caves.

We didn't ask how Strike had come to that conclusion. Somewhere in his vast databases he had specifications for every Starnavy vehicle. No doubt he'd used them to work out where the shuttle was going. It was the sort of thing which machine intelligences did 'in the blink of an eye' as

Bahar put it. Strike didn't have organic eyes, but you get what I mean.

Now I want you to go up there, he told Howin.

Surveillance, or intercept? she asked.

Surveillance, initially. Until we know more. But I can't help thinking those False Manifesto people might come back there, and if the hostiles hide out, they could end up running into them.

Without any warning, Howin replied. *Not good. Okay, we'll start climbing now.*

Strike sent his drones to accompany the squad. I watched the troops climb for a while, until I was distracted by a snow lion creeping along in a gully at the base of the mountains. It froze, then pounced on something grey. After a brief struggle, the grey thing stopped moving.

The snow lion ripped into the creature's belly with its claws, and the creature's insides spilled out. The drone images picked up steam from them. I'd never eaten such things, but the snow lion gobbled them up.

Alert, Strike said over the feed, wrenching me away from my study of the animal. *Troops just disembarked from that shuttle. They're wearing armour. And... yeah, they're starting to climb the northern side of the mountain.*

"Will our people reach the caves before they do?" Bahar asked.

"Should do," Strike replied. "Just got some intel on their shuttle. It dropped from the *Crimsonstar*. Picking up coms now, and they're not using standard Starnavy IDs or protocols."

"Why?" I asked.

"Because the protocols auto-record the data. If you want it off the record you need to remove the headers." Strike would know, of course. He must do that often when speaking to Unit contacts. But the Unit had its own recognition codes too.

"That's worrying," Bahar said.

"It is. I've sent Howin a hurry-up," Strike replied. "Sending drones over to get a good look at their shuttle."

"I'm thinking about the *Nebulafire*," Bahar replied. The *Nebulafire* was a Starnavy frigate which had gone rogue and attacked us at Reeva. "Is there an organisation of these rogues about?"

"You mean, a corrupt Special Investigations Unit?"

"That's an interesting way of putting it. But... yes, I guess I do mean that."

"It hadn't occurred to me to search for one, but I'm starting a search now." Strike zoomed his drones in on the figures climbing the northern side of the mountain. "Their armour doesn't bear any Starnavy logos."

"Now why am I not surprised by that?" Bahar asked.

We watched Howin and the troops reach their target cave. *Hold there,* Strike said. *Sending drones in first.*

Acknowledged. Howin's voice was calm, and she didn't even sound out of breath.

Strike put up a feed on the wallscreen from one of the drones. The image darkened as it entered the cave, then it engaged its low-light filters. It flew inside, and we saw empty passageway beyond it. It entered an empty cave at the top of the passage.

Clear, Strike said over the feed.

Howin drew her pistol and went into the cave. The drone view showed the troops standing just inside the entrance. They were waiting for their eyes to adjust to the darkness before engaging the night vision filters on their helmets. Humans had poor night vision. Mine was good. Strike said I had a thing called a 'tapetum lucidum' in my eyes, which reflected back the light.

Going in now, Howin said over the feed, and started to climb up the passage. *Is this passage natural?* she asked.

Can't find any planetary files on exploration there, Strike said. So he'd been snooping around again. I wasn't surprised by that either. *Potential hostiles are climbing fast. Looks like the northern ascent is easier.* There was a touch of worry to his mental tone.

Don't fret it, Strike, Howin replied. *We'll get there.*

The drone ahead of her reached the topmost cave. *There are three side caves where you can hide*, Strike said, and sent the locations into the feed.

Okay, let's get in there, Howin replied.

The troops picked up their pace, and 5.7 minutes later they came out into the topmost cave.

Projected route of potential hostiles is your location, Strike sent. *Get into cover.*

Howin swiftly detailed the troops to split up and hide in the side caves. 3.3 minutes later they were all out of view from the main cavern.

Cover's good, Strike confirmed. *Stay there. Drone feeds coming over.*

He settled the drones up by the roof of the main cave. He angled them to give views of the passages from the north and the west.

Potential hostiles definitely coming your way, he said.

Ten minutes from you.

The view from the drones in the cave didn't show any visual evidence of the troops. A thermal scan might, though. They had to stay quiet and hidden and not draw attention to themselves.

I found that kind of waiting tedious. I could do it. I was a lion, after all. Lions spent a long time stalking, and waiting for their prey to get into range. But I didn't enjoy waiting. It was boring.

The drones' audio brought us the sound of boots on rock, and the occasional click as armour and weapons moved.

Hostiles in cave now, Strike sent over the feed. The drones there showed six armoured figures, with rifles live. *Looks like Starnavy kit. Weapons are new. No logos on the armour, but that's recent issue too.*

So our President's outfitting his hit squad with the best gear? Bahar asked.

Looks like it. Audio from their suit coms coming over now.

It was a rough, hissy line. Strike had hacked their suit coms, of course. "Remind me again why we're doin' this?" That came from a male human. He was a full head taller than the rest.

"Because the President wants us to find evidence these people are traitors, remember?" That voice was a woman's, full of exasperation.

A second man replied, a deep voice that rumbled as he laughed. "He'll make up evidence if we don't find any. We know what his agenda is."

"And we know what we signed up for," tall man replied.

"Yeah. A big, fat bonus that'll bring my retirement forward ten Standards," the woman said.

"Wasn't planning on scrabbling around mountains to get the dosh," deep-voice grumbled.

"Quit bitchin, and search," tall man ordered.

"This is the scary bit," Bahar said.

I could hear her breathing turn ragged, and her scent had a thread of fear to it. Strike could order the drones to shoot the intruders if necessary, but it would be much better if the troops remained undetected.

"Nothing here," deep-voice said.

"Conversation's interesting," Strike said. "Recording. This is a private operation financed by Jorrak. Didn't think he was that wealthy. I wonder where the credits came from."

"I sense more Unit investigations," Bahar replied.

"Already under way."

Right. I should've expected that. Of course Strike would think about that. 'Follow the money' he always said.

To my great relief, the hostiles didn't search the side passages. The troops were tucked out of sight around curves in those passages, and not visible from the main cave. Strike's drones would definitely have investigated them, but this bunch didn't have drones with them. They peeked into the openings, but didn't venture further.

Sloppy searching. The scorn in Strike's voice was clear, mixed with a touch of relief. *They're retreating. Yeah, they're done there. Going down the northern side of the mountain again. They're trying to decide what to tell Jorrak. Definitely on their way back to their shuttle. The light's beginning to go. Think you'd be better off sleeping there tonight,* he told Howin. *Don't think you'd reach the half-way cave before dark, and there's a snow lion patrolling those slopes.*

It could get up here, Howin replied.

You can put up shields across the cave mouths. It wouldn't cross them.

True, Howin replied. *They'd be a dead giveaway to those hostiles, though. Hope they don't come back.*

CHAPTER NINE

I went to sleep in the shuttle a short while after the troops bedded-down in the cave. There was nothing I could do to help either Merrill or them, and I was tired.

When I'd settled myself, Strike opened a private feed line to me. *This hit squad bothers me*, he said. *They'll go looking for False Manifesto somewhere else now.*

Get the Unit to look out for them.

Already sent that instruction. Strike's tone held that familiar mixture of exasperation and indulgence.

So why are you bothered by them?

Because Merrill's disappeared. If the Predatorbot Programme has been halted, she might be one of the people who worked towards that. If Jorrak knows it, she'll be one of his prime targets.

I... hadn't thought of that, I said. Now his fretting made sense. *What can we do about it?*

Nothing. That's what's bothering me. All we can do is send out warnings, and wait.

When I woke it was past dawn, and Strike said the weather was on the turn. He'd had to explain that expression to me. Human language has so many ridiculous sayings. Strike used them without any problems. Only me, the uplifted lion, had a problem understanding some of them.

Anyway, this time he meant the sunny autumn weather had turned cool, and the sky was grey this morning, and getting what he called 'threatening'.

The troops had started their climb down the mountain at dawn, while I was still asleep. As soon as I'd finished my meal I joined Bahar in the control room, to watch the drone images Strike was streaming to the wallscreen.

The troops were still high up on the mountain. "Howin says coming down is more challenging than going up," Strike told us. "They're moving much slower. She says the terrain is treacherous."

I remembered when I'd first discovered that going downhill could be harder than going up. It was when I was six months old, and we cubs had been taken out on a training exercise. We'd got stuck at the top of a steep ravine. I'd eventually made it down safely, but two of the cubs had been badly hurt in falls. I never saw them again. It was only later that I learned the techs had killed them.

So I believed Howin, is what I'm saying, and Strike did too.

As the short autumn day wore on the dark threatening clouds began to change to a curious white sky. "Don 't like the look of that," Bahar said.

"I don't either." Strike's voice was tinged with worry. "I calculate it's going to take the troops at least another hour to reach the shelter of the half-way cave."

"And you think the snow might start first?" Bahar asked.

"Yes. Sending the troops a heads-up."

The snow started to fall half an hour later. Within minutes, the sky was filled with white.

We have a problem, Howin said. *I can't see anything. I'm afraid we'll miss the cave.*

Stand still, Strike ordered. *I'm sending a drone over to you. Reach out and grab the line it's extended.*

Howin put out one hand in front of her, and after some groping she closed her glove around the line. *Got it*, she said. *Passing the line back now.*

Strike waited until everyone had secured it to their armour. *The drone can see through this. Trust it to guide you down*, he said.

Acknowledged. Howin's voice showed a touch of strain for once.

"None of the weather sats forecasted this. I should've

seen it though," Strike said to us.

"*Thunderstrike* the supermortal," I replied. "Able to do things no other mortal can."

"That's…"

"No fighting," Bahar said. "Don't be rude, Snap. It's not always possible to plan for every variable in advance, Strike. You know that. You're dealing with this."

"The troops are still in danger."

"They'll survive it." Bahar sounded more confident than her scent suggested.

After a tense hour the drone stopped at the cave entrance. The visual from the other drones around it showed only feint thermal traces. The white-out was complete.

You've arrived at the cave, Strike sent over the feed. *Put out your right hands and feel for the wall. The drone will lead you inside.*

Acknowledged. Howin's voice betrayed the faintest touch of relief.

Let me do the scans before you bed down, Strike said. Howin released the line, and Strike sent the drone off to scan the space. *Clear. It'll be officially dark in ten minutes. Get yourself settled.*

Out of the wind, Howin said, and led the troops around to

the sheltered space they'd used on their way up the mountain.

They settled down to eat and sleep, and Strike returned to his worrying. "The President's troops got away," he said. "The snow's much lighter on the other side of the mountain. And Corradino's weather forecast is for a full day's snow tomorrow. Our troops are going to be stuck there for another day."

"Then they are," Bahar replied.

"You don't understand." Strike's annoyance showed in his voice. "I've lost track of the President's troops. And we don't know what happened to the False Manifesto people here. This mission has been a disaster."

CHAPTER TEN

The storm raged all the next day. Howin and the troops opted to stay in the cave until it blew itself out.

Part-way through the day a snow lion came sniffing at the cave entrance. Howin had put up a force shield to keep all the creatures out, and the snow lion stopped before it touched the barrier.

I think it was smelling the energy discharge from the generators, and maybe even hearing the whine from the units too. To my relief, it was cautious, and chose not to risk injury. It snarled in annoyance at not being able to use the cave to shelter from the storm, then turned and picked its way down the path.

"Poor beastie," Bahar said. "We stole your shelter."

"It'll survive," Strike replied. "It has thick fur for that. Not like Snap."

"I was bred for heat," I replied. "I don't like snow."

Bahar laughed, and reached down a hand to stroke my neck. "I don't like snow either. My ancestors were bred for heat too. So, Strike, can we do anything useful today?"

"I can. My drones have picked up the trail of the President's troops again. Now they've sent their drones in to investigate the caves. Mine are shadowing them. I really hope they don't find anything there."

Despite Strike's fretting, the drones found no trace of False Manifesto in any of the caves. But instead of calming Strike down, that made him more annoyed. "I should've been monitoring shuttle launches," he said. "They probably left as soon as we arrived."

"Don't fret it," Bahar replied. "The Unit will pick up their trail somewhere. They're not going to fade away with the Presidential campaign just kicking off."

"You're right. Okay. I'll try to contain my impatience."

As evening fell the snowfall slackened off. *Corradino weather forecast predicts fine weather in the morning*, Strike told the squad over the feed. *Tomorrow you should be able to get out of there.*

I slept well that night, and woke after dawn. Strike told me the snow had stopped falling six hours ago, and the thaw had started.

The troops were already on the move, and a couple of hours later they reached the base of the mountain. *Glad to be off that slippery trail*, Howin said as the troops came onto the rock where the shuttle had landed.

We're glad you're back too, Bahar replied.

The troops came aboard the shuttle 5.4 minutes later, and suddenly the passenger compartment was full. Howin lounged in her seat and said, "Now what, Strike? Do we hang around here, or look elsewhere for Merrill?"

"Plan change, as of now," Strike said. "The hostile shuttle just launched. They're on their way back to the *Crimsonstar*. My guess is they're going to leave then."

"So are we leaving too?" Bahar asked.

"You are. Sealed up. Systems checks complete. Lifting you now. Going to keep you off their tail, though. Don't want to alert them to our presence."

"Don't they know you're up there?" Bahar asked.

"They can see a large debris collector on their scans. It's about to finish picking up debris from a security system unit failure."

"Which never happened," I said as the shuttle's drive fired.

We lifted through the planet's atmosphere. I flattened my body to the deck and tried to ignore the press of g on my body. I still didn't really understand how gravity worked. Through the viewport I saw the shuttle climb above the planet's clouds and into black sky.

"Hostile shuttle's definitely headed for the *Crimsonstar*," Strike said. "You're staying on the other side of the planet. And you're going inertial now."

The drive cut off, leaving us floating in space with only the occasional thruster burst to maintain our orbit. 10.7 minutes later Strike said, "And… hostile's just gone aboard the *Crimsonstar*. Bringing you aboard now."

Strike piloted our shuttle into his vehicle bay as efficiently as always, and landed it square on its pad. "Where do we think the *Crimsonstar* is going?" Bahar asked as Strike shut down the systems.

"Just intercepted their coms. They're going to Kyoko Station."

"So they don't want the local Commander to know they were here?" Howin asked.

"That's my reading."

"What do you want us to do now?" Rance asked.

"Freeze-down," Strike replied. "I shouldn't need you for a while."

"Okay, will do," Howin said. Nobody objected to the order. The troops got restless with nothing to do. They preferred coldsleep to boredom.

Strike confirmed the hold was aired-up, so we left the shuttle. Bahar let the troops go first, and I was last. It was good to stretch my back as I padded across the deck.

The troops went up in the lift first. Bahar and I went to the galley. I was hungry, and Bahar said she was too. So Strike fed us while the troops went to the cryobay.

That was how he kept Bahar out of Howin's way while they got into their pods. Bahar would fuss over them, and Howin would get cranky about her fussing, so it was best to keep the two apart.

Strike fed Bahar a spicy stew that made my nose twitch. I wouldn't like that at all. I much preferred my haunch of juicy raw marissa meat. It was printer-produced, of course. Strike didn't keep live prey aboard.

"And… the *Crimsonstar* has just gone into jump," Strike said as we ate our meals. "Destination's definitely Kyoko. We're on our way there too. I've sent advance notifications to the Unit there."

"Are you expecting trouble?" Bahar asked.

"I can never be sure my aliases haven't been rumbled. It's always best to plan for the worst."

That… wasn't reassuring. Why did I get the feeling Strike knew something he wasn't telling us?

The jump to Kyoko was a long one, and Bahar and I had reached the usual stage of terminal boredom long before we emerged.

Strike wanted us both in armour for downjump. "So what are you worried about, Strike?" Bahar asked as his drones helped her into her armour.

They'd already put mine on, and I shook my pelt to settle it comfortably over my back.

I often get flashbacks to the Programme at times like this. The Programme's armour for Predatorbots had been badly-designed, and it rubbed my skin after I'd worn it for a few hours. That's why I hadn't wanted armour when I first came aboard Strike.

Strike had insisted on it. He'd had his drones measure every part of my body, and then he'd promised that the armour he got for me would be custom-designed, and would be comfortable. He'd delivered on that promise.

I don't know where he got it made, but let's just say that (a) petbots don't usually wear armour, and (b) their artificial coats don't usually have a camouflage facility. No doubt Strike had used some Unit contact to get it done.

Bahar and I returned to the control room and Strike said,

"I received a Unit heads-up while you were on Ennor. They think Jorrak sympathisers may have worked their way into major positions on Kyoko Station."

"So why are we only hearing about this now?" Bahar asked.

"Because I didn't want you fretting all the way here."

I wondered how Strike dealt with keeping secrets sometimes. Sapient machine intelligences had all the emotions. He didn't often show fear, but I knew he experienced it. How alone did he feel sometimes, keeping such secrets locked up inside his processors?

That was not a productive thought, as Nyla would say. Thinking of her brought my anxiety back. The more people challenged Jorrak, the more danger Nyla would be in. I hope we find her soon.

"Downjump in ten minutes," Strike said.

I tried not to notice his extra systems checks of his shields and weapons. If Bahar noticed, she said nothing about it. She did fidget in her seat though, and her scent was low-level anxious.

"Downjump in three… two… one…"

Strike had given us a short countdown. I wondered if he sometimes got tired of us meatbags overreacting to things.

The scene through the viewport changed to black space and stars. We'd downjumped successfully. "Uh-oh," Strike said. "Unit's intercepting coms from hostiles. Someone's issued an order to kill me."

He was trying to keep his voice light, but his fear bled through. "Luckily, the *Furyfire* and *Stormblood* are here. Lei's just allocated them to station defence, and sent them our way." Lei was a machine intelligence in Kyoko Station Security, and she was part of the Unit. As were the *Furyfire* and *Stormblood*. Strike would have allies around him here.

"Now we just have to hope our reinforcements reach us before trouble erupts," he said. "I have permission to put shields up and go weapons hot." That meant Strike thought the threat was serious, and Station Security agreed with his assessment. "Getting nav update now."

On the plot, a red dot started flashing. Strike estimated it had come in from Darray Station, and he'd passed a request through our Unit contacts here to check things out there. That was the strength of the Unit. It had people everywhere, and could pull in data from thousands of contacts.

"*Thunderstrike*, we think the *Bloodknife* is making for you." The voice was a young human Traffic Controller's; a male, and sounding frightened. "We're clearing the sector around you."

"Acknowledged, and thanks," Strike said.

"There's a second blip," Bahar said. Her scent spiked with fear.

Strike was unruffled. "Yes. They haven't seen it. It's stealthed. *Stormblood*, what's your status?"

"I'll be there in time," Blood replied.

"Weapons hot," Strike said. Red lights came up on the consoles in front of Bahar. She checked them, but of course, Strike would be firing the guns.

"And now they've gone to weapons hot. Adjusting course." Strike moved so that he was behind the *Bloodknife's* main guns. The stealthed ship was holding back, clearly not going to engage us at this point.

"Is the stealthed companion the mop-up ship?" Bahar asked.

"I think that was the original plan. But they didn't expect me to have reinforcements," Strike said as *Stormblood* came up beside him. "Now we'll see if that alters their plans."

CHAPTER ELEVEN

I was conscious of Bahar's ragged breathing, and the touch of fear in her scent as we waited for the potential hostiles to act.

"And… Station Security ships are on their way out to escort them into station," Strike said. So he'd been hacking Traffic Control's coms again. "Companion's not hanging around. It's running. Let's see if I can get an ID from it. Starnavy protocols being rejected. By a Starnavy ship. I could force it to tell me who it is, but… Sending scan and com data on to the local Commander."

"Why didn't you demand its ID?" Bahar asked as we resumed our line in to station.

I knew why. Strike would've had to force his way into the machine intelligence's deepest memories. Strike said that was the machine intelligence version of what humans called rape. He wouldn't do it unless ordered.

"Because I didn't." His voice was firm. Bahar got the message, and shut up.

Our approach to dock was normal, and Strike filed a report about the engagement with the local Commander as he docked.

"Good news. The Commander doesn't want a briefing with you," he told Bahar. "So you're free to go on station and meet our contacts. See if you can find out what the hostile reception was all about."

So it had bothered him. Strike's unruffled persona was showing cracks.

Bahar and I went on station an hour later. Strike said there was a subtle tension to the place, but he couldn't work out why. I wore my armour, retracted as usual, and this time I'd set it to a shimmering blue. Bahar said looking at it was unsettling. I hoped that would direct attention away from me.

When we set foot on the dock it was busy. Two troop carriers had just arrived, and were sending their people ashore. Bahar got off the dock at the closest lift lobby, and we stepped into a car before the troops could all crowd in there.

Why so many troops on an off-Spine station? Bahar asked Strike over our feed line as the car took us up.

I was wondering why too, I said. Most troop movements used the Central Spine stations. Kyoko was a way off it.

Something to ask our contacts when you meet, Strike

replied. That meant he didn't know.

The lift car let us out on the leisure level. The lobby here was busy, and I kept behind Bahar as she cleared a path for us out to the hallway. Thankfully, once we'd reached it the crush thinned out. I'd managed to arrive on the footway without getting my nose bumped this time.

"I wonder what interesting stuff we'll learn today," Bahar said as we walked along. She was meeting our contacts at yet another café. This one specialised in Black River fusion food, whatever that was.

I became aware of a gold blur in my peripheral vision. Gold blurs usually meant lions, and here that most likely meant a Predatorbot.

Don't react, Snap, I told myself. I was a lion; my instincts were to focus on anything that moved. But if it was a Predatorbot, and I reacted to it, it would immediately realise that I was one too. Don't look round. Ignore it.

What's wrong, Snap? Bahar asked over our feed line.

Right. That meant my body had tensed up. Take a deep breath, Snap. Relax.

I think there's a Predatorbot here, I said. *Look to your left.*

Bahar stopped walking and pretended to be interested in

a display of jewellery in a shop window. She slowly and casually turned her head to the left, then back to the display of jewellery. *I think you're right*, she said. *Let's get to the café. You acting the dutiful petbot should bore it silly.*

It's trying to access my behaviour module. Sending me a recognition code.

Don't respond, Bahar said. Now her voice was tense, and her scent had turned anxious. Her stride lengthened, and I trotted beside her along the hallway. Ahead of us, I saw another female lion appear. It stood on the footway, waiting for us to approach.

Hello, Snap.

The voice in my feed startled me, but I managed to stop my body flinching.

It's Lei. I saw the Predatorbot, and I came over to help, she said.

Relief flooded my body. This was Lei's avatar. I walked forward and rubbed heads with her. *I'm glad you came*, I replied.

Predatorbot's studying us, she said. *We'll have to pretend to be petbots for a while. Let's get to the café.*

Bahar took the lead, and Lei's avatar padded along the

hallway beside me. It was a good copy of me. You couldn't tell which one of us was the organic lion unless you touched us.

We didn't talk while Bahar led us to the café. That told me Lei was worried about our coms being hacked. I was too. There was no knowing what other awful tech had been shoved into Predatorbots' bodies since I'd escaped from the Programme.

We reached the café. The concierge exclaimed over the 'two beautiful petbots', and fussily led Bahar to the booth where Berj and Andula waited for us at the back of the café. Both contacts were human, white-skinned, and middle-aged.

"Glad to be rid of him," Lei said as the concierge walked away. "Creep." So she thought so too. Maybe my judgement of humans was improving.

Bahar greeted our contacts, and the humans spent 9.7 minutes discussing what they wanted to eat. I know they have to cook their meat, but seriously, why do they need to disguise all its sweetness with sauces so spicy they make their eyes water? I'll never understand them.

I'm checking out the café, Strike said over our feed. *Don't want you caught in some surveillance sting.*

Bahar said nothing while Strike's drones did their work.

Clear, he said.

Lei engaged the booth's privacy shield. I knew that wouldn't make the space private, but Strike's drones hovering above us, and Lei's links, would.

"What's the news around here?" Bahar asked.

"Was hoping you'd tell us that." Lei said. "What was that attempted intercept of *Thunderstrike* about?"

"Strike said a kill order had been issued for him. We're assuming it was those two hostiles out there."

"Oh. Not good," Andula said. She worked in Starnavy Logistics Branch. "I'll ask around casually. See what I can find out."

"So there was a stealthed ship with the *Bloodknife*?" Lei asked. Her voice betrayed worry. "We weren't sure."

"Yes, but Strike doesn't have an ID on it. And when *Stormblood* came to join him, potential hostile ran for the jump point."

"That's worrying," Berj said. "We couldn't resolve the issue of whether a second ship was really there." Berj worked in Kyoko Station's Traffic Control. I saw a brief expression of disappointment cross Bahar's face at his words.

"Act casual, Snap," Lei said. "The Predatorbot's just

come in here. It's with a trooper, and I think it's trying to borrow your trick of pretending to be a petbot."

"Then how do you know it's a Predatorbot?"

"Because it's scanning for security contacts. Not going to give them that information."

The Predatorbot and its handler hung around for an hour, checking people out. The trooper ordered a sandwich, and casually glanced around him as he ate.

When he'd left the café Lei said, "We've had orders to report every sighting of a Predatorbot direct to Central. The Unit's been doing some careful digging around on that order's coms path, and guess what? Those reports get prioritied to President Jorrak."

"Is he planning to use them to help him cling onto power?" Bahar asked.

"Interesting idea," Berj replied. "Hadn't thought of that."

"Or to suppress dissent and inconvenient facts," Andula added. "Either way, it's not good news."

Our contacts didn't have any more useful information, so after Bahar had finished her lunch, we returned to *Thunderstrike*. The dock was quiet now, all the troops gone ashore, and we reached *Thunderstrike's* berth without any problems.

Welcome back, Strike said as he opened the lockout gate for us. *Come to the control room. I have some news.*

Oh, we were in mysterious mood again, were we? Strike had paused after that announcement, expecting us to ask what his news was.

Bahar didn't take the bait. *We're on our way up*, she said, and led the way to the lift.

Strike kept quiet until we got to the control room. I had the feeling he was annoyed with us. This was all the usual nonsense, which told me everything was fine. I settled in my place beside Bahar's seat, and asked, "So what's the news?"

"First, that the sighting of you on station was sent to our President."

"What?" Now he'd got a reaction from me. "Why didn't you..."

"I did block it." Was there a touch of satisfaction in his voice? It bristled my nape fur. Strike must've seen it, because when he spoke again all traces of smugness were gone. "It's a worrying development. I've sent out a general bulletin to everybody in the Unit. We'll have to be very careful what you do in future."

I had a surge of anger, and snarled. "I didn't choose to be

a Predatorbot. How long am I going to have to keep hiding? How long will I be at risk?"

CHAPTER TWELVE

Half an hour later Strike received orders to take essential coms supplies to Diandra Station. He couldn't refuse the orders without arousing suspicion, so he was forced to take the assignment. It would send us off the Central Spine route, and I could tell that Strike was annoyed about it.

I went to the control room before the loaders arrived, and Strike locked me in there. He put up vid from his two port holds onto the wallscreen for me, to watch the action down there.

"They're not wearing Starnavy Logistics uniforms," he said. "The design is close, but the colours are off. And they have no insignia."

Bahar had gone down to the holds to meet the loaders. Instead of their usual banter, this crew interacted stiffly with her. That wasn't usual. *Is something wrong here?* she sent over our feed.

I can't find anything wrong, Strike replied. *The equipment seems to be standard coms components. And it came from a Starnavy bonded warehouse.*

So we go ahead with the loading? Bahar asked.

I can't find a good reason not to, Strike replied.

Whether the loaders were official or not, they were efficient, and Strike's cargo was loaded fast. His drones crammed the cargo in tight, giving no access to the packages at the far end of the hold. Why had I thought of that? Strike's tension was infecting me now.

The loaders left, and Strike began his systems checks. I noticed he scanned the cargo three times for software traps and power sources. Nothing came up on any of his scans.

We got our line out, and Strike said, "Undock now. We have a fast run out to the jump point." The way he said it, I wondered if he still suspected something was wrong. It wasn't helped by him sending his drones down to 'check that the cargo was properly secured' before we went into jump.

As we were lining up for jump, he received a file from an unnamed Unit contact. He ran his checks for malware and killware, and said, "File's clear. I think it came from Lei, but I can't be sure. Opening it now. Oh."

"What?" Bahar asked sharply.

Strike put the text of the message up on the wallscreen. <From your friendly lion. Rumour has it that a certain Commander is a close friend of KJ.>

"What does it mean?" I asked.

"It means the Commander at Kyoko is one of Jorrak's

cronies," Strike replied. "I do wish Lei had sent me this before I accepted the cargo."

"You don't think there's something bad there, do you?" Bahar asked.

"I arrive here to find some mysterious person has put out a kill order on me. I file a report on it, and the local Commander doesn't want a briefing about that very serious threat to me." Strike was angry now. "Then I get cargo loaded by people with the wrong uniforms on, and… Yeah, I do suspect something bad's going on."

"Okay, you've made your point," Bahar said. Her eyes were wide with surprise, and her scent had a spike of fear to it.

I was surprised by Strike's outburst. This wasn't the supremely confident, snarky, clever, machine intelligence I knew. This sounded like a small, scared person.

"So do we say there's something wrong and return to station?" Bahar asked. "Fake a fault, so we can get into dock and get the Unit to check out the cargo?"

"We could, but what if that's what the Commander wants us to do? What if this is some elaborate sting to unmask the Unit?"

"And maybe you're overthinking this, Strike," Bahar said.

Strike went quiet for 3.7 minutes after that comment. Then he said, "I may be," in a quiet voice.

"So are we going for jump?" Bahar asked.

"We are." His voice was calmer now. "We're already so far behind Merrill, wherever she's gone. We can't afford another delay."

Strike was quiet as he made his way out to the jump point. Just before we reached it he said, "I've been stripping docking lists from Kyoko. There are four fast Starnavy cargo haulers in dock there. Two of them don't have filed flight plans."

"Your point being?" Bahar asked.

"My point being that they could've been assigned to take this cargo to Diandra. In one case, departing sooner than me. So why wait for me?"

"I don't know. Strike, you just have to make a decision here," Bahar replied. "Are we going, or are we not?"

"We are," he said. "Countdown to jump beginning now. Let's hope it's the right decision."

Our entry into jump was normal, and for the first 5.7 hours everything was calm. I was just thinking about going to sleep when Strike said, "We have a problem."

"What?" Bahar asked.

"I'm reading energy discharges from the holds. Small ones, but a lot of them."

"So what are they?" I asked.

"Oh. Now we have a really big problem," Strike said. "Analysis of the signals shows they're trackers. Someone wants to know where we are. They must've been on delayed timers. How could I miss that?"

"That doesn't matter now," Bahar said. "What does matter is disabling them."

"There are 227 of them."

That… was a lot of code to disable.

"We have to turn off every one of those trackers before we downjump," I said.

"You grasp the scale of the problem," Strike replied. "It's going to take both of us to get this done in time, and it'll be close."

CHAPTER THIRTEEN

Strike showed me what to look for, and we started in on disabling the trackers. Except that Strike wanted to do more than that. He wanted to send a power surge to each unit and fry the transmitter.

I could do that, but it made me exhausted very quickly, and I could only work for four hours at a time. I fell into a sound sleep after each work session, but Strike would only let me sleep for four hours each time. So I was still tired when I woke up.

Strike made me work fast, and I knew from that he was scared. Was this the next move of whoever had issued that kill order on him? Had they tried to make sure we wouldn't survive next time? I'm sure Strike thought that.

The nearer we got to downjump, the faster we worked. Thankfully, the trackers weren't smart code, and they weren't talking to each other, so we could use the same attack to destroy each one.

One hour before emergence Strike said, "We're done. Reading no hostile signals from anything now."

"Thank the universe," Bahar replied.

"Let's hope there's nothing else rogue in there which I

haven't spotted."

"And let's hope we don't downjump into an ambush this time," Bahar replied.

I said nothing. I was too tired to talk. I laid my head on my front feet and fell instantly asleep.

I woke to the sound of Bahar's voice. I opened my eyes and blinked the bleariness away, then raised my head. I was sprawled out on the control room deck. Out of the viewport I could see black and stars. So we'd downjumped okay. I was surprised I'd slept through transition, but I had been utterly exhausted.

"Welcome back, Snap," Strike said. His voice was soft and calm.

"Did we…"

"Downjump was normal. And no, we hadn't missed anything. No trackers turned on, no hostile reception party."

I yawned, and shook my pelt. "That makes a change."

"Sure does," Bahar agreed.

Two blips were coming towards us on the nav plot. "Are those hostiles?" I asked.

"For once, not," Strike replied.

I blinked, and focused my eyes on the labels by the dots.

Arrowfire and *Furyfire*, they read. Those were two Starnavy frigates. Was that good or bad?

"I contacted Roza as soon as we downjumped," Strike said. Roza was a Unit machine intelligence in Diandra Station Security. "She ordered those two to escort me in. I reported the trackers on my cargo to the local Commander. Hence approval of the escort. She's worried about those trackers, and she's impounded the cargo. We're getting Starnavy Investigators to take them off as soon as we dock. Our escort's coming into position now."

On the nav plot, I saw *Arrowfire* and *Furyfire* change course. One came up on Strike's port side, the other on his starboard. They matched his speed, and the three ships made their way into dock.

"We're going to be noticed," Bahar said.

"If that gets us into dock safely, I'll take it," Strike replied. That's when I knew he was still worried.

I watched the nav plot for a while, but nothing hostile came towards us. We were on a fast transit in, but even so, we wouldn't get into dock for many hours. I yawned, and Strike said, "Go get some comfy sleep, Snap."

"I think I will," I replied.

He let me into my quarters, and I settled down into my

bed. I was still wiped out from those too-short sleep periods.
I curled over on my side and closed my eyes.

"Sweet dreams, Snap," Strike said as I sank into sleep.

I woke ten hours later, feeling properly rested at last.
Strike fed me in my quarters, then I went to the control room.

Bahar was in her seat. The bruised look had gone from
her face, so she'd had some real sleep too. "Morning, Snap,"
she said.

"Morning, Bahar. So how far out from dock are we?" I
asked.

"Twelve hours. And… oh, just got an alert," Strike
replied.

"Knew it couldn't be that easy," Bahar grumbled.

"The *Firefist* is off its line. It's a Starnavy troop carrier.
And… we're being ordered to change course."

"Is this the next attack?" Bahar asked. Her calm scent had
turned anxious.

"That would be unwise," Strike replied. "We have Arrow
and Fury with us, remember? I don't think they'd be stupid
enough to take on three frigates. Altering course now."

I watched the nav plot as Strike and his escort looped
around the troop carrier's course. I'm sure Strike expected

an attack from *Firefist*, but it didn't come. 12.2 hours later Strike eased into dock.

"Getting a contact from Starnavy Investigators now," he said. "They're wanting to come aboard right away."

"So you need me in my quarters?" I asked.

"I do. They'll want to come to the control room and check my logs."

Was there a touch of nervousness in Strike's voice? In theory, everything he did should be recorded, but the Unit wouldn't have survived for even one Standard if he did that.

I knew he'd made alterations to what he called his 'Unit memories', cutting them off from commands entered via the control room's consoles. The only people who could access those memories were Strike and me. There was no record of the partition in his files, and to anyone checking his systems, those memories showed up as empty.

I went to my quarters and settled down in my bed. I hated this wating alone while Strike did risky things. And having Starnavy Investigators come aboard was a risk for us.

The Investigators were three black-skinned human males, dressed in the dark grey uniforms of Starnavy Investigation Branch. Strike put vid of them up on the wallscreen in my quarters.

The investigators sent their own drones in to examine the cargo. They swooped in close, and stuck patches to the boxes. "Looks like they're finding contact DNA," Strike said. "Idiots forgot that it only takes a few skin cells or a hair to identify them."

The drones spent an hour recording images of the cargo and taking samples from the boxes, then the loader bots went in to move the cargo. The Investigators left without finding anything useful or suspect in Strike's logs. I could sense his relief as he saw them walk down his ramp.

"They're taking the cargo to an Investigation evidence warehouse," he said. "I've been digging around here, and nobody knows anything about an urgent shipment of coms tech. I suspect the Kyoko Commander will shortly receive a visit from Investigators."

"If he's still there," Bahar replied. "He'll probably know by now that the attempt to kill us failed."

"True," Strike said.

"So what now?"

"What now is that Diandra's local Commander does want a debrief with you. So I'm afraid we're not finished with this incident yet."

Bahar put on a uniform and went onto Diandra Station alone. That made me anxious, which was ridiculous. I was supposed to be a heartless killing machine, yet here I was, fretting about not being able to protect Bahar. Those idiots at the Programme had no idea what they'd created.

Strike's drones accompanied her to the briefing, of course, and when she arrived the Commander wanted Strike to join the discussion too.

"Which is good," he said. "She won't notice me streaming data out if I'm officially part of the discussion." He meant the feed he was sending to the wallscreen for me.

I settled on my belly and watched the conversation. No, Strike's cargo hadn't been requested by anyone here. Yes, an official investigation was under way.

"I'm wondering if this is somehow connected to the *Firefist* failure," the Commander said. "The ship suffered a loss of helm control an hour after downjump here. You said the trackers you found on your cargo turned on after a delay, Strike?"

"Yes. They were triggered by our entry into jump."

"Is it possible something like that was at work on the *Firefist*?"

"I think that's unlikely," Strike said. "It would have to be hostile code inserted into the ship's operating systems to affect helm control like that. That's radically different from someone bringing a hostile cargo aboard."

I wouldn't fancy the chances of anyone trying to insert hostile code into Strike's systems. Since Chan had attacked him he'd become ultra-cautious about what coms and data he accepted. He'd sent a report of Chan's attack to Starnavy HQ, heavily edited so that it didn't mention my involvement in that near-disaster. Strike said the Starnavy had made some coding changes to protocols since then. He also said they were nowhere near as robust as the defences he'd constructed for himself.

"What worries me is that the *Firefist* is only one Standard out of commissioning," the Commander said. "She's a brand-new ship, and that sort of catastrophic failure shouldn't happen."

"I certainly agree with that," Strike said. Was that a touch of fear I heard in his voice? Maybe. He'd become more aware that people could kill him after Chan's attack. Strike had changed since Chan died. Bahar said he'd got a glimpse of his own mortality.

Some of the first sapient machine intelligences were now a century old. Strike said there were some Starnavy

Commanders who always asked for centenarian machine intelligences to join their divisions. They valued those intelligences' long wisdom. Strike was only half their age, so I guess it was reasonable for him to fret about his life being cut short.

"I hesitate to suggest this, but I wonder if the incident was linked to our President," Strike said.

Careful, Bahar sent over our feed line. What was Strike up to now?

"In what way?" The Commander's question was neutral.

"I've heard a lot of rumours about our President making personal contracts in the Outliers. I'm wondering if he had a hand in this too. If he could recruit a troop carrier and its crew for his personal projects he'd have a serious resource."

"Are you suggesting the loss of helm was part of a mutiny attempt?"

"It's a possibility. I'd suggest Investigative Branch interviews the crew when the ship gets into dock," Strike replied.

"I'd planned to do those interviews, but in view of what you've just told me I will turn it over to Investigations. Is there anything else useful you can tell me, Strike?"

"I don't think so."

"Then you're all dismissed. Go get some downtime," the Commander said.

Bahar returned to *Thunderstrike* immediately after that debrief. I'd like to think she felt nervous on station without me by her side, but I'm sure that's just what Strike called 'vanity thinking'.

She came aboard an hour later, and went to the rec area for coffee. I joined her there. She flopped into a seat and took a swig of her drink. "I'm assuming you saw all that?" she asked.

"I did," I replied.

"Do you think they'll start to investigate Jorrak now?"

"I hope so. I'd already sent Investigations Branch a file before we talked to the Commander. From one of my aliases, of course. Hopefully they'll put all these reports together and seriously investigate him," Strike said.

"What if they find nothing wrong?" I asked.

"Then that's fine. I'm not out to destroy the man. I just want to see that he's operating fairly and legally. Oh, Roza's sending me a file," he said. "You might want to see this." Video came up on the wallscreen. "She says this was recorded on Offir."

The file was a drone record of a False Manifesto rally on the planet. "Why has Roza sent this… Ah," Bahar said.

"That's why," Strike replied. He froze the image and magnified it. "That's definitely Merrill. So she got out from Ennor, and she's still with those people."

"And still working in the background," Bahar observed.

"So are we going to Ataret Station next?" Bahar asked. Ataret was the closest station to Offir.

"We are," Strike said. "I'm annoyed with myself for not monitoring shuttle launches from Ennor. Merrill must've left the planet before the troops even got to the mountains."

"But if they hadn't gone there, we'd never have known for certain that the President had his own troops. The evidence they collected there is valuable."

"I… you're right," Strike replied. "Okay, maybe it wasn't a complete disaster. And at least Ataret is only one jump away. Requesting a departure slot now."

CHAPTER FOURTEEN

Strike called in some favours from his Unit contacts on Diandra Station, and got a fast refuel and resupply arranged. As soon as that was finished Traffic Control contacted him to offer an earlier departure slot. Strike took it, and two hours later we were leaving Diandra.

"No cargo this time. No trackers," Strike said.

He'd sent his drones into his holds immediately the Investigations people had removed the last of his cargo. He said he wanted to be sure there weren't any other nasty surprises lurking there. He hadn't found anything.

I kept my attention on the nav plot as he manoeuvred out of station, but nobody approached us, and there was nothing out of place. I hoped that would hold when we reached Ataret.

The time out to jump was filled with a boredom we hadn't experienced for a while. It was a welcome change from attacks and danger, but it meant I had nothing to stop me fretting about Merrill. The files Roza had sent Strike showed two False Manifesto rallies on Offir. They'd been violently broken up by thugs wearing armour with no logos. Strike suspected they were the President's personal troops. So far,

Merrill had avoided being harmed by them, but it only took one facial recognition scan to identify her as Nyla's sister and that would change.

Offir was closer to Central. Were False Manifesto working their way there? That would increase the danger for Merrill. And for us.

I was glad when we downjumped at Ataret and I could fret about something else. Now I worried about us being attacked on the way in, or us being attacked on station. It was exhausting, and this heartless killing machine was glad when Strike locked onto the dock.

"Alert," he said as he started his power-down. "Tyger's sent me a warning. Six frigates have just downjumped here. They came in from Pekado, and he thinks they're travelling together as a strike force. The ships don't bear the Starnavy logo on their hulls."

"So what are they?" Bahar asked.

"Tyger thinks they might be part of our President's personal forces. He seems to be amassing quite an army." There was a touch of anxiety in Strike's voice.

"You're thinking they might be after False Manifesto?" Bahar asked.

"I've got no evidence of that."

"You want us to go on station?"

"I'm still checking out whether it's safe for you."

That meant Strike was hacking into station feeds. And that Tyger was making sure nobody noticed his surveillance. It would get harder to do that the closer we got to Central. I was hoping we caught up with Merrill before then.

"I think you'll be safe enough on station," Strike said, interrupting my gloomy thoughts. "I want Snap to wear her armour, and for you to wear a deflection vest, Bahar." So he wasn't entirely convinced the station was safe. "Tyger wants to meet you in a secure conference room."

"Which will be secure by the time you've finished with the feeds," Bahar replied.

"Indeed."

"Then we'd better get moving," I said.

Tyger's avatar was already in the conference room when we arrived. It took the form of a tiger with blue and silver iridescent stripes. "Welcome back to Ataret," he said as we walked in. The harsh overhead lights made his stripes shimmer.

"It's good to get into a station without being attacked for

once," Bahar said.

"Yes. Strike worried everyone with his report of trackers on his cargo. Hopefully we won't get caught that way again."

"They'll just try something else," I said.

"They might, but we'll be checking more carefully in future. We're getting to the stage where we can't trust that every Starnavy ship is keeping to the codes," Tyger replied.

"The sooner we vote this President out, the better," Bahar said.

"You're assuming that will happen. False Manifesto are doing their best to discredit him. They're stepping up their campaigns now the Presidential race has officially begun. I've sent Strike a whole stack of files which we received from Iku recently." Iku was a planet close to Aadanna Station, and relatively close to Earth. "Strike's doing his own analysis of them, but I think they indicate that False Manifesto has a base on Iku."

"What do you know about those six frigates that just downjumped here?" Bahar asked.

"They're worrying. They always give us advance notice of a task force of eight-plus ships. I can't help feeling this smaller group is an attempt to avoid being noticed," Tyger said. "We're trying to find out why they have no logos on their ships, but nobody's talking. Traffic Control are pushing for security guarantees for station from the task force Commander. Station hasn't quite accused them of being rogues, but they've made their disquiet known.

"They're splitting the ships up, so they're berthed on different levels and at different locations. We're doing what we can to make it harder for them to organise."

That wasn't exactly reassuring, but I suppose it was the best station could do. Tyger and Bahar talked of several other things for the next hour, but nothing Tyger knew helped with our search for Merrill.

"I'm thinking Snap and I ought to be on our way to *Thunderstrike* now," Bahar said as she finished her third cup of coffee.

"I agree," Tyger said. "Everything's still calm, but you want to be back aboard before trouble erupts. It's been good to catch up."

"I'm going to set my armour to hideous again," I said. "Cue a cute petbot disguise coming up."

When we left the conference room I'd programmed my armour to show cartoon lions walking all over it, on a bright green background. The colours clashed horribly, and Bahar said that should help her to go unnoticed too. After all, nobody important would own a petbot with such a hideous coat, would they? I tried not to feel offended by her comment.

We crossed the station to *Thunderstrike's* berth just after the start of station's Third Shift. The busyness of shift change had gone, and the hallways were relatively quiet. Well, as quiet as the halls of a Central Spine station ever got. We'd spent so much time off the Spine in recent Standards that we'd got used to quieter stations.

I tried to stop my ears twitching every time I heard something. That was a dead giveaway that I was a lion. Fortunately, nobody took any notice of us.

Strike let us through the lockout gate. As we cane into the airlock he said, "Come up to the rec room. I've a file I want you to see." There was no hint of mysterious mischief in his voice this time. He sounded… worried.

We rode up in the lift to Deck Two, and Strike had a mug of one of Bahar's favourite coffees ready for her when she arrived. She took it from the dispenser, flopped down in a seat, and said, "Show us this file, Strike."

"Tyger sent this fifteen minutes ago. He's just received it from Iku."

The wallscreen lit with a high-level view from a drone camera. The drone was hanging over a large square. Tall buildings with the look of business headquarters lined two sides of it. Hotels and cafes filled the rest of the space. At one end of the square someone had constructed a stage. Large banners with the False Manifesto name flapped in the brisk breeze. The banners had a logo of a man's head in silhouette, with a red lightning strike through it.

"Is that my imagination, or is that head supposed to be Jorrak?" Bahar asked.

"I believe so," Strike replied. "Clever using a silhouette. They can always say it isn't him if he turns nasty. I've been analysing their campaign speeches. They've never outright accused Jorrak of corruption. They just campaign for honesty and openness in government."

"Leaving people to draw their own conclusions as to who's not honest," Bahar said.

"Indeed. Watch the end of this."

The rally ended in an attack on the speakers. Black-clad men wielding shock batons leapt up onto the stage and started hitting people. The scene quickly became a riot, with people running everywhere.

Strike blanked the wallscreen. "The thugs got away, of

course."

"What about Merrill?" Bahar asked.

"That's the worrying thing. She doesn't appear in any of the files of their later rallies.   She seems to have disappeared."

"Are we going to Iku to look for her?" Bahar asked.

"We are. We'll be leaving for Aadanna Station in twelve hours' time."

Bahar and I went to get some sleep before we left station. I came back into the control room just before our departure time. Bahar still hadn't appeared.

"Lots of activity from station," Strike said. "All sorts of advisories coming over. Including warnings about riots on Iku."

"Any news of Merrill?" Bahar asked from behind me.

"No. I think Tyger's right about False Manifesto having a base on Iku, though. A lot of their coms are coming from there. They're trying to mask the originating location, but they're working with civilian gear. Starnavy can easily find out where they are."

"Or Jorrak's rogue forces?"

"Yes." Strike's voice held a tinge of worry. "Starting

undock procedures now."

He eased away from the dock with his usual efficiency, and turned onto his outbound line. "Alert," he said. "Got an advisory that those six frigates have just requested outbound slots. Tyger thinks they're bound for Iku."

"Then it's good that we'll arrive before them," I replied.

CHAPTER FIFTEEN

We went into hyperspace on schedule. The jump was a short one, but even so, it was long enough for us to reach our usual stage of boredom.

Twenty hours before downjump Strike secured a private feed line to me and said, *I'm worried.*

I was in my quarters, napping in my bed. I raised my head and asked, *What about?* I was not in the mood for a dose of Strike's angst right now.

I've been doing systems checks, and I can't decide if there's something in my scan systems that shouldn't be there.

That woke me up. *Why aren't you sure?* I asked.

Because every time I run a diagnostic it turns up something different. Sometimes there's a ghost of something there, the next time it doesn't show up at all.

Now I was worried. *You think there's hostile code lodged somewhere?*

I do.

Then we have to find it, I said.

Strike's plan was to let me into his architecture and for me to lurk there while he did his systems checks. He thought the code had a smart component that was reacting to his presence in the systems. If I just sat there watching, maybe I'd be able to find it.

He'd written some new delete code for me, which he said was hard to spot before it struck. I wouldn't know. Coding was a machine intelligence thing. They had their own protocols and languages, most of which I didn't understand.

I settled back down into my bed. If I was going to do something which exhausted me, at least I could be in a comfortable place while I did it. I closed my eyes, and Strike opened a pathway into his architecture for me. This feeling that my consciousness had left my body never got any less unnerving, but it was familiar.

I settled in to watch Strike work. His strings of code whispered through my consciousness like searching tendrils, seeking for the weeds which were growing in his systems. That's the way I'd described this process to Bahar once. I was possibly the only meatbag being who had any idea what it was like to be a machine intelligence.

A flurry of code leapt up from one of the external scanner inputs. I tagged it – and it turned on me. It was trying to access my memories. I deployed the new code Strike had written for me, but it didn't destroy the invader. It took out part of it, but wow! What was left was fast, faster than my defences. I had to shut down my machine half before this hostile destroyed my memories.

Shutdown initiated.

Snap.

Something was whispering through my mind. Why couldn't I shut it out? This hostile code was attacking me, and I couldn't…

It's me, Strike. I've purged the hostile code from your systems. You're safe. Wake up, Snap.

I opened my eyes. A blurry scene of greys and blues gave me no clue to where I was. I blinked, and the room came into focus. Oh yes, I remember now. I'm in my cat bed. I was helping Strike to drive out hostile code.

Did we… I said over the feed. Moving my jaw to speak out loud was still too much effort.

I got the hostile. I tore it apart. The savage note in his voice made me shiver. I sat up and shook my pelt. My body ached like I'd… I was going to say like I'd chased prey for hours, but I don't actually know if that would feel like this. I've never chased prey.

Whatever. It was what I always felt after I'd been in

Strike's architecture. I was utterly exhausted.

We're six hours from downjump, Strike said. *Get some sleep.*

I settled down in my bed and closed my eyes. And tried not to worry about the tension I heard in Strike's voice.

I woke an hour before downjump. Strike fed me, and didn't scold me for being a messy cat. That told me he was still worried about the hostile code.

I went to the control room and settled into my space beside the captain's seat. Bahar had arrived before me, and as I lay down she stroked my neck.

"Are you rested, Snap?" she asked.

"I slept well enough." But now that I was awake I was fretting again about that hostile code. Strike hadn't been able to figure out its function before it attacked me. He'd done two full systems checks since he'd destroyed it, but I knew he was still worried about it. Bahar had picked up on Strike's tension too, and her scent had turned anxious.

"Downjump in three… two… one…" Strike announced.

His voice had a touch of fear to it. I felt the same. I was remembering those trackers we'd had to disable, and wondering if this hostile scan code was somehow connected to them. And wondering whether something else would turn

on when we downjumped.

CHAPTER SIXTEEN

Bahar's anxiety-scent was strong as we downjumped. I was just as bad. My right hind leg twitched. I moved it, flexing the muscles and easing the tension.

Through the viewport the roiling greys and reds changed to the serenity of black and stars. So we'd downjumped okay, but was Strike okay?

"Not reading any anomalies," he said. Was that relief I heard in his voice? Yes, it was. So he hadn't been entirely sure he'd got all the hostile code out. I thought so.

"Oh. I'm being asked by Traffic Control to send my full Starnavy ID."

"Haven't been asked for that for a long time," Bahar said. "I wonder what's happened to get them to request it."

"We'll find out later. Sending ID now."

Strike's full Starnavy ID was a file with several codes in it. It was deep-coded into his memories, in a location with no identifier tags. Stations didn't usually ask for that data. Strike's name and ship class was usually enough for them. Which meant that Aadanna Station Security was worried about something.

"ID accepted. We have our docking assignment," Strike

said. "Going in now."

The nav plot came up on the screens. It looked normal, with a straight line in. It was busier here than we were used to, but Aadanna was closer to Earth, and this was normal traffic for here.

"All incoming coms are being scanned by Station Security," Strike said. We didn't ask how he knew that. A Unit contact must've tipped him off about it somehow. "I'm not making contact with the Unit until we dock," he said.

I agreed that he needed to keep quiet, but it meant that we were going into station without any of our usual warnings. We wouldn't find out about any problems until we docked. I'd forgotten how much we rely on our Unit contacts to keep us out of trouble.

It was a normal approach and docking. As soon as we locked onto the dock Strike contacted our Unit people here. We didn't have anybody in Station Security as part of the Unit at Aadanna. It was too close to Central, and its security procedures were tougher than the Outlier stations. Trying to recruit contacts in Security or Traffic Control here carried too big a risk that the Unit would be exposed.

So our contacts here were in civilian positions. Bahar

treated them as if they were personal friends she hadn't seen for a while, and arranged a casual meet-up at a café in one of Aadanna's big parks.

She dressed in a robe decorated with tribal designs. It wasn't as fine as the outfit she'd worn when she was kidnapped, but it was bright enough to make her stand out. I was going with her, and I set my armour to a brilliant scarlet. I guess we were doing that thing Strike called 'hiding in plain sight'. After all, if you drew attention to yourself, you couldn't be plotting something bad, could you?

We were meeting Chaye, a human Station Administration manager, and Hyordis, a human who worked in Logistics on station. We were joining them at a café in one of Aadanna's curious red-leaf parks. I found it hard to imagine living on a world where all the grasses were red. My golden pelt colour was supposed to camouflage me against the golden grasses on Earth's savanna. When the green grasses dried out and turned golden, we were perfectly camouflaged. If I lived on a red-leaf world I wouldn't be a very successful hunter.

Our contacts were sitting at a table right on the edge of a terrace. Chaye had skin as dark as Bahar's, Hyordis was very pale, with golden hair. Chaye saw Bahar approaching, and waved to her. We wove our way between the tables on the terrace, and Bahar sat down. Our contacts were dressed in bright leisure clothes too.

"So, what's the news?" Bahar asked after her coffee had been delivered.

"We keep gettin' files from Iku from these False Manifesto people," Chaye said. "'M thinkin' they have a base down there."

"Strike thinks so," Bahar replied. "We're looking for Merrill Vatan, who seems to be working with them. She looks like this." She sent a couple of images of Merrill over to their implants.

"Haven't seen her around here," Hyordis said. "False Manifesto were quite open about having a base on Iku until a Standard ago. They published the address as their campaign HQ. But recently that's disappeared."

"Have been some big rallies on Iku recently," Chaye said. "Lotta support for False Manifesto there, an' it's growin'. Got a feelin' there's gonna be big trouble on Iku soon."

"Why do you think that?" Bahar asked. Her scent had turned anxious, shot through with fear.

"'Cos our President's turnin' sour, an' he knows they're gonna expose him. Gotta make sure they don't get him voted out, ain't he?"

"Strike's warned us about that too," Bahar said. "He's not joining our discussion here because Station Security were scanning all incoming coms when we arrived. I think he suspects they might be scanning coms on station too."

"He's right to be cautious," Hyordis said. "False Manifesto people on station are being followed around. It's almost bad enough to count as harassment, but not quite. I suspect this kind of thing will get worse the closer we get to the election."

Our contacts didn't have any more news, so Bahar and I returned to *Thunderstrike*. The lift lobbies on this station were bigger than we were used to, and noisier too. We had to wait for 5.8 minutes for a free car. As we walked inside and the doors closed I saw Bahar's shoulders drop.

"Well, that was a nice catch-up, wasn't it, Snap?" she said. She spoke in that brittle-bright voice she used when she was pretending I was a petbot. It was a warning to me not to say anything incriminating.

"It was," I said, making my voice equally bright.

Bahar sighed. "I do wish we could meet up with our friends more often, but I suppose I should've thought about that before I joined the Starnavy."

Thankfully, the car reached its destination then, so I didn't have to think up a reply to that. Bahar led me out into the lobby, which was full of troops in fatigues noisily talking about what they were going to do on leave. I dropped back behind Bahar, to avoid getting my nose bumped.

The dock we came onto was just as busy. Even though *Thunderstrike* was only one berth away from us, it took us 31.7 minutes to weave our way through the troops and reach his lockout gate.

Strike opened it for us, and Bahar stepped onto his ramp. "Glad to be out of those crowds," she said as she came into the airlock.

"Me too," I replied as Strike closed the outer door behind us.

We walked to the lift and Strike brought us up to Deck Two. As we came into the control room Bahar asked, "How's things, Strike?"

"Station's just received this," he replied.

He put up a file on the wallscreen. A tall, white-skinned woman with long blonde hair appeared on it. "She's Bryssa Meir," Strike said. "Presidential candidate. I've cut the tedious bits out of her speech."

Bryssa wore a black pant suit, and she paced as she spoke.

"It is time for change," she said. "For too long the Outliers have been treated as second-best by this Administration. Some colonies have recently been denied essential supplies. This is not how things should be. The Collective Charter gives everyone equal rights – to resources, and to voting. I have received many messages from Outlier citizens recently, who fear that their votes will not be counted in the upcoming Presidential election.

"If I am elected, I will ensure that the Charter's provisions are adhered to. I will make sure that the Outliers receive the representation they deserve. If you vote for me, I will ensure equality for everyone."

The wallscreen blanked, and Bahar said, "Fine words." There was a touch of sarcasm to her voice. "We've heard all this before." I knew Bahar had suffered discrimination because she has dark skin. I could see why she was sceptical about Bryssa's words. Discrimination against their own species is something I'll never understand about humans.

"Yes, we have," Strike said. "But False Manifesto are officially backing Bryssa. And they're gaining members every day. There's a chance she could be front runner."

"So how does this help with the search for Merrill?" I asked.

"It makes it even more important that we find her. If Jorrak sends his troops in against False Manifesto…"

"Point taken," Bahar said. "So where are we going now?"

"Iku, of course," Strike replied. He put another file up on the wallscreen, of a big False Manifesto rally. "This was in the capital there, only two days ago."

Bahar leaned forward and studied the images. Then she pointed at a figure on the wallscreen. "Is that Merrill?"

The woman in the image was in view for only seconds, then she disappeared. Minutes later, shots could be heard, somewhere on the fringe of the crowd. Panic gripped the people, and the crowd ran away, screaming, as snipers fired at the stage.

Strike blanked the wallscreen. "Luckily, nobody was killed in that attack. Iku security arrested some of the snipers. They refused to tell them who they were working for. They're in detention down there until they talk. The weapons they were carrying look like Landforce issue. None of the snipers were wearing uniforms, and they didn't carry any identifying effects. I'm sure they're Jorrak's thugs, but nobody can prove that."

"Merrill's in danger down there," I said.

"Everybody's in danger down there," Strike replied. "I've

put in a departure request to station, and our troops are in wake-up. We're going to Iku to find Merrill."

CHAPTER SEVENTEEN

We left Aadanna Station an hour later. Our line out to jump was busy, and Strike had to travel at minimum speed. It would take us three shipboard days to get into jump.

I fretted all the way there. What if there'd been another rally and Merrill had got shot? What if she was dead?

I didn't know Merrill, but I knew Nyla would be devastated if her sister died. She and her sisters had been very close before they'd had that massive row about the Programme.

Strike thought they'd now be prime targets for Jorrak's squad. He'd already arranged for more security for Fia and Rhian on Davion, and he was having Zana's ship tracked and shadowed by Unit members.

Someone was continuing to release old files about the Predatorbot Programme, and Strike thought Nyla had a hand in that. And with Merrill involved with False Manifesto, the danger to the sisters had increased. We really needed to find Merrill and Nyla soon.

I was glad when we reached the jump point and went into jump. I hadn't commented on the fact that Strike had done a full systems check on the way out, but it told me he was nervous. The jump was short, and we emerged into a region of space busy with Starnavy ships.

"Don't like the look of this," Strike said. "Why is there such a big Starnavy presence here?"

"Maybe they've been sent to protect the False Manifesto people," Bahar replied.

"Optimist." Strike wasn't convinced.

"They're not in orbit," Bahar pointed out. "They're just… hanging about in local space."

"You're right," Strike replied. "Let's hope they stay there."

As Strike eased into orbit around Iku we had some luck. "*Fireblazer's* here," he said. *Fireblazer* was a Unit ship. "Getting a data dump from him now."

"Ask him about Merrill," I said.

"Already done."

Well, yeah. I should know better than to second-guess Strike. He could do things before I'd even finished thinking about them.

"Blazer thinks she's still here. False Manifesto are holding a large rally in Kareela tomorrow. That's a regional town on the smaller continent. So guess where you're going," Strike said.

"I'm going too," I replied.

"There might be Predatorbots down there. What if they notice you and report on you?" Strike objected.

"Which is just why I should go. I know the kinds of strategies the Programme taught us. And if there are Predatorbots down there, maybe I can turn them."

"Dreamer," Strike replied, but there was affection in his voice, not scorn.

"It takes one to know one," I said. "You…"

"Stop it," Bahar cut in on our conversation. "I'm not in the mood for your bickering right now."

I turned and gave her a hard stare. She stared right back at me, and I realised that was another reason why I liked her. She wasn't afraid of my fierce female lion self. She knew I was much more than that, and she made me live up to my potential.

"Okay, so Snap goes with the troops," Strike conceded. "But you'll be keeping your armour on all the time."

That would be irritating, but I could see why he'd insisted on that. "Agreed," I said.

"I'm going down to check on the troops," Bahar said.

Strike let her out of the control room, and closed the door

after her. "She's edgy," he said.

"She's afraid of Merrill getting killed. Like me," I replied.

Strike went quiet for 5.7 seconds, then he admitted, "It is a possibility. But I don't want you getting killed there either."

I didn't know what to say to that. I'd never even considered the possibility. This was Strike showing his love for me again, and now I felt ungrateful.

"I'm making a hotel reservation for you in Kareela," he said, breaking into my musings. "I can't leave the shuttle at the 'port for the troops. There's too much traffic, and it's a small 'port. So you're going to have to be ordinary travellers for once."

"Troops in armour don't look like ordinary travellers," I replied.

"They'll look like farmers in from the country. Howin won't like it, but tough."

Bahar reappeared. "Howin's awake, and hungry. Like me. Feed us, Strike."

"Go to the galley," Strike replied. "I suppose I'd better feed messy cat too."

"You sure had," I said. "You don't want me biting people because I'm hungry."

"You wouldn't dare," Bahar replied.

"No, I wouldn't. You humans taste tough and sour."

She gave me a startled look. "How do you know that?"

"I had to bite a chunk out of your kidnapper's arm to get him to let go of you. I don't want to eat human."

Bahar's expression was a mixture of shock and surprise, then she trailed her fingers along my neck and said, "I'm sure glad I'm on your side, Snap."

I didn't know what that meant. Howin joined Bahar, and did her ritual complaining about the wake-up drink Strike made for her.

The humans settled down to eat, and I devoured my meal. By the time we'd all finished the rest of the troops were awake and had gone to the rec area. Strike was busy briefing them when we walked in.

He was right about Howin's objection to their disguise. They would be wearing armour, but they'd have bulky field gear over it. I knew Howin hated that.

"I've got a landing slot at Kareela spaceport for two hours' time," Strike said. "So you need to eat quick, then load up."

I stayed in the rec area with Bahar while the troops got settled in the Xenophon. Then she and I went down to sit in the shuttle's control room, as usual.

"Leaving now," Strike said.

The vehicle bay airlock slid open and the Xenophon exited *Thunderstrike*. Iku lay below us. The night side was turned towards us, the positions of settlements showing up from the patterns of light down there. A lot of the interior of that continent was dark.

We dropped, coming into atmosphere as we crossed the terminator into the dayside. Kareela shuttleport came into view below us.

"Got my landing slot," Strike said. "It's a lot busier there than I expected. I've booked you a 'taxi to take you to your hotel." He sent over the booking details. I stored them in my memories. "And no complaining that it's not five star."

I didn't know what that meant, so I just watched the shuttle drop towards the 'port. Strike took us down as expertly as always, and landed the shuttle 'feather-light', as Bahar called it, on the pad.

The 'taxi arrived and we got into it, the troops sprawling in the seats at the back. They tried to look like casual civilians, but there was always an edge of danger to them, a hint that they were something more.

The 'taxi took off, making its way into Kareela's centre.

The city was bigger than I'd expected, with a number of skyrakers. Being in those made me nervous, and I hoped we weren't going to one now. Lions are meant to roam free over vast grasslands, not be locked into metal towers.

10.2 minutes later the 'taxi pulled up outside what was, thankfully, a low, sprawling complex of buildings. We got out, and Strike said, *You're in the Sunrise Lodge. You have it to yourselves.* He sent a map of the complex to us.

Bahar went inside and dealt with the human on registration. She returned clutching six keycards. Handing them out, she said, "Strike's been extravagant here."

It wasn't my credits, Strike said over the feed.

That was one of the morally grey things Strike did. He said he 'grabbed resources from greedy megabillionaires who'd never notice'. Yes, Strike, the defender of the Collective's Charter, is also sometimes a thief.

We sorted ourselves out, and Bahar and I claimed one of the suites, with Rance and three of the troops. The others dispersed to claim their spaces.

Okay, Strike said over our team feed when we'd got settled. *The shuttle's in a park ten minutes' walk from you. Here's the location details.* A map and route came into my mind, and I stored them in my memories.

The rally you're interested in starts at noon local time, in Discovery Square. That's here. Another map came over the feed, and I saved that to my memories too. *You have a couple of hours to get there and check out the place before the rally begins.*

I know a hint when I hear one, Howin replied. *We're on our way over there now.*

Discovery Square was already busy when we arrived. The square was the usual mix of offices, glossy shops, cafés, and restaurants. Bahar and I went to a café. The troops dispersed around the square, checking out likely sniper spots. Yes, Strike was expecting trouble at this rally. I really hoped Merrill was still okay.

Bahar drank coffee as we waited for the rally to start. Coffee had turned out to be one of those plants easy to establish on other worlds, and had spread throughout the Collective. That was lucky for Bahar. I don't know how she'd survive without it. She was addicted to the stuff.

Crowds gathered in the square, and by noon it was jammed full of people. At five minutes past the hour a tall black man strode onto the large permanent stage at the square's southern end. The crowd erupted into applause. He raised his hands, and the square fell silent. Bahar and I hung back at the edge of the crowd and watched the scene via the livestream Strike's drones sent to our feed.

That's Jamar Talmai, Strike said. *He's the front man.*

The rally was the usual fare of accusing Jorrak of being useless, and claiming that only Bryssa could right things. Strike said they weren't Bryssa's official campaign team, but it sure looked like it.

Towards the end of Jamar's speech Strike said, *Merrill's there. Behind the stage. She's feeding data to the screen. Oh. Trouble.*

It happened fast. One minute the crowd was chanting Bryssa's name, the next people were screaming as shots rang out.

On it. Howin's voice came over our feed. *Got the first sniper.*

Got a second. That was Rance. *There's still a third out there somewhere.*

The third sniper had a line of sight to the stage, and was putting shots onto it, riddling the banners with holes. Jamar and the others on the stage dived for cover and shots slammed into the lectern where he'd stood moments before.

Iku security got him, Strike said over our feed. *Don't*

think there are any more hostiles.

Where's Merrill? Bahar asked.

Strike went quiet for 4.7 minutes. *I can't find her*, he said. *She's disappeared.*

Did she get shot?

I don't think so. Strike sounded annoyed. *I should've kept a drone focused on her. I didn't. I lost her. I'm sorry.*

Strike didn't often apologize for things, and it shocked me – and scared me. It meant that he thought he'd messed up – and that Merrill might've got hurt.

Time for you to head back to your hotel, Strike said. *Iku Security are starting to arrest people. You don't want to get caught up in that.*

No, we don't, Bahar said. *Come on, Snap.*

Your 'taxi is here, Strike said, and sent a route map to our feed.

On our way, Bahar replied.

We left the square and turned into a narrow side street crammed with people. 6.2 minutes later, somebody stepped between me and Bahar.

"Got one," a woman said. "Let's get it back for examination."

Someone tried to slide a collar around my neck, and I

realised they were after me. *Help*, I sent over our team feed. *I'm being kidnapped.*

CHAPTER EIGHTEEN

"What the hell d'yer think you're doing?" The shout startled me, and I flinched. It was Howin's voice, and she stood right over me. "Get your hands off my petbot, you thick tossers!" She sounded angry, and she'd put a lilt into her words I'd never heard before. Oh, right. This was Howin pretending to be a farmer or whatever.

"We thought it was our petbot we lost a Standard ago. It looks the same," the man said.

"Yeah, sure. Move, creep," Howin snarled. "Don't wanna have ter beat you up to get my property back."

The man swore at her, then obviously thought better of it. It was infuriating staring at their waists. I couldn't figure out what was going on.

He's leaving, Howin said over our feed. *We're going too.*

She moved off, and I stuck close by her side. The advantage of being with Howin was that she had this magic ability to clear people out of her way, and it worked just as well this time.

Where's Bahar? I asked as we reached the end of the road and came out by the 'taxi pickup points.

Already aboard the 'taxi, Howin replied. *We're joining*

them now.

She stopped by a vehicle and someone opened the door for us. I jumped inside. "Are you okay, Snap?" Bahar asked.

"I am. Howin rescued me."

"Some tosser claiming Snap was his lost petbot," Howin snarled as the 'taxi moved off.

"Do you believe that?" Bahar asked.

"Don't know. Need to be on our guard for more snatches, I think," Howin replied.

I caught the warning in her eyes not to talk about it, but Howin obviously thought we might meet more trouble here. Oh, that was really going to help me sleep well tonight.

We hung around the hotel complex for the rest of the day while Strike tried to find out what had happened to Merrill.

Howin discovered some old Starnavy buddies of hers were in town, and went off to spend the afternoon with them. Rance and the rest of the squad stayed around us, having swimming competitions in the hotel's pool, and getting ultra-competitive at several games involving throwing hoops and rolling balls.

Bahar and I chose to stay on the hotel's terrace and watch them. It didn't escape my notice that Rance had detailed two of the troops to be always close to our table to watch us.

At dusk Bahar and the troops ate in one of the hotel complex's restaurants. Howin still hadn't returned. Half-way through our meal she contacted us to say she was on her way back.

Strike had spent the afternoon hacking into medical admissions records for Iku's hospitals. He reported on his searches when we returned to our rooms after dinner. *I can't find any trace of Merrill in the planet's medical records*, he said. *I've done a face recognition match on the records too, and nobody looking like her was admitted this afternoon. She's just disappeared.* He sounded annoyed. *So unless something new turns up in the morning, you might as well leave there tomorrow.*

The 'something new' turned up at 2 a.m. in the morning.

Strike sent a wake-up tone through our feeds. As I yawned and tried to get my brain to work Strike said, *Someone's trying to break into the hotel complex.*

It might not have anything to do with us, Bahar said. She yawned, and began pulling on her clothes.

Oh, I think it does, Strike replied. *Sending you the conversation now.*

The voices were feint, with a slight hiss on the line. Strike was relaying them via his drones' inputs.

"You sure it's here?" That was a man's voice, deep, and sceptical.

"Tracked it in." That was a woman.

"What's he want 'em for anyway?"

"Keep him in power if things go wrong. Can't lose, can he?" The woman's voice was full of scorn.

Does she mean... Bahar fastened her deflection vest.

Jorrak? Strike replied. *Pretty certain she does.*

"Why do I care?" The man asked. "They're all as rotten."

"I care 'cos he's paying us good credits. Got it? Goin' in."

They're through the outer gate, Strike said.

A drone image came up of a tall man and a burly woman. *Not wearing armour. Both armed with heavy-duty pistols, but they're civilian weapons.*

So we think Jorrak sent them to grab Snap? Bahar asked.

That's my reading.

Bahar slipped her jacket on over her vest and dipped her hand into its pocket. The pistol she brought out was Starnavy issue, and could easily kill someone.

Oh, now they're hacking into the guest list, Strike said.

Won't find us there, Bahar replied.

I did have to reveal that you were Starnavy and would be carrying weapons. Sorry, Strike replied. *The security scanners would've alerted on you otherwise. I guess they're targeting you because you're most likely to have a Predatorbot.*

Which is true, Howin said, entering the feed conversation.

Looks like they're coming to your room first, Bahar, Strike said. *Get Snap out of sight.*

I'm going, I replied.

The room had a bathroom large enough to fit me into, and I padded inside and Bahar pulled the door part-closed on me. My anxiety spiked. I was leaving her alone out there to face those two armed thugs.

They're trying the lock on Bahar's door, Strike sent over the feed.

Can't you lock them out? I said.

Howin's in place. Going to let them in and see what they say.

"Got it." The man's voice was stronger now. An image from a drone came up in the feed, of the man using some kind of tech on the door lock. The feed switched to the one from the drone inside our room as the door opened.

Bahar stood on the other side of it, fully-clothed, and

pointing a pistol at the intruder.

"What do you want?" she snarled. "Jamil, call Security. We got an intruder. Now why are you here?"

"None 'o your business," the man snarled, which was about the most stupid thing he could've said.

"It's my business when armed thugs break into my hotel room at 02.10 a.m."

The man blinked at the precise timing, and I could see him reassessing Bahar. His female accomplice came into the hallway from the other direction.

"I'll ask you again. Why are you here?" Bahar said.

A drone from the hallway showed me Howin striding towards the hostiles, her pistol drawn. "Get away from there," she snarled, using her 'farmer' voice again. "Just move along an' I won't call Security on you."

The man swore at her, took in her serious pistol, then flicked a hand signal to the woman. They turned and walked away down the hall.

Sending intruder report in now, Strike said. I knew that would be a cleaned-up version of the incident, without any reference to petbots. *Tracking your thieves. Oh, they're getting into an armoured skimmer round the back of the complex. Moving off now. Looks like they're going to a shuttle park.*

They were, and Strike sent us drone images of the skimmer going into the vehicle bay of an unmarked shuttle. *That's a Starnavy vehicle, but it has no badging. All indications are this is part of Jorrak's squad. Shuttle's not leaving, so I think we'll see more trouble from them soon.*

CHAPTER NINETEEN

We woke late the next morning after our night-time disturbance. After a hearty breakfast in one of the hotel's cafés, we left Kareela.

Strike sent a 'taxi for us, and it took us to the shuttle. "You're relocating to Yerrodin today," he said when we'd all got aboard. Yerrodin was Iku's capital. "There are a couple of Unit contacts in town. I want you to go meet up with them, Bahar."

"Okay, take us there," she replied.

Strike guided the shuttle out of the hangar and we turned north and flew out over a large ocean. By the time we reached Yerrodin it was dawn there. The morning was fine, and the first fingers of starlight lit up the edges of the buildings in dazzling highlights.

Yerrodin Shuttleport dealt with our arrival efficiently, routing us away from the drop pads to the perimeter of the 'port. "Managed to get you secure parking here," Strike said as he guided the shuttle around a network of roads to a small hangar. He took it inside and said, "'Taxi's ordered. It'll be around ten minutes."

By the time we'd made it out of the hangar the 'taxi had

arrived. It took us around a maze of one-way streets and dropped us off in the middle of the central business district, with tall skygrazers all around us.

"We're not going into one of those, are we?" I asked, swinging my head around to indicate the nearest structure.

Bahar bent down and stroked her fingers along my neck. "Don't worry, Snap. We wouldn't do that to you. Strike says we've got a ground-floor meeting room."

You're going to the New Horizons Business Centre, Strike said in our feed.

I've lost count of the number of New Horizon facilities I've been in, Bahar replied.

I could calculate it. If I got bored enough one day, Strike replied. *But it's a lot. You humans are so predictable with your names. This one's a small facility. I know Snap doesn't like skygrazers.*

No, I don't, I said. *Thanks, Strike.* He was looking out for me again, and it gave me a strange, warm feeling in my chest.

The business centre looked shabby compared to the glossy skygrazers which surrounded it, but it had a homely feel to it. Why do human business places all have to be unwelcoming hard plas and shiny metals? Bahar says it's something to do with macho posturing, whatever that is.

Here are your registration details, Strike said, and sent a name and codes over the feed.

He'd booked us in as the directors of a bogus company, being very vague about what that company did. Bahar said that didn't matter. She couldn't understand the corporate-speak of most of them, and neither could most people.

Our two contacts met us in the building's lobby. Kaatje was the captain of an independent civilian freighter called the *Fargold*. The human woman had bronze skin, and copper hair tied in a thick braid. Strike said her ship was small, and she made a good living doing small deliveries which the bigger shiplines 'turned their noses up at', as he put it.

Our other contact was Tarian, a short white-skinned human male. He was in Station Security at nearby Oriela, and here on leave. The humans did the usual greeting-and-getting-drinks thing, then they settled down to talk.

"Things are getting pretty tense on Earth," Kaatje said. "Riots happening regularly now. False Manifesto people are being arrested and harassed – and they're making a great deal of noise about it. Hardly a day goes by without someone accusing Jorrak of some fraud."

"How much of that is the usual political posturing?" Bahar asked.

"Some, certainly," Tarian replied, "but there are things I don't like going on there. I have orders to observe False Manifesto. Given that they're a legal organisation, that bothers me."

"Do you think there'll be a move to make them illegal?"

Tarian shrugged. "Who knows? I guess it depends on how the Presidential election campaigns go. There's one other thing you should know." He looked down at me. "We've been ordered to report any sightings of any cats which might be Predatorbots, priority to Central."

"Where are those reports going?" Bahar asked.

"I asked around, casually. Turns out they're being sent to our President. And no, I won't be reporting Snap. That damned Programme should never have happened. I'm not gonna help that man kill innocent creatures."

"You think that's what he'll do?" I asked.

"I strongly suspect he will. Remove the evidence of his evil doing, so he can hold up his hands and say 'not me' when it comes to election time."

"Bastard," Kaatje snarled. "We need to be rid of that man."

Tarian didn't comment on that. "The good news is that I've heard rumours that the Predatorbot Programme has been suspended until after the election," he said.

"That's something, I suppose," I replied.

Our meeting broke up at noon. Bahar and our contacts ate a leisurely lunch at a casual café down by the Nishan River, then Bahar and I went to find the hotel Strike had booked for us.

Howin appeared at the end of the first road we turned into, and waved casually to Bahar. Bahar strode towards her. I sensed she was relieved to have backup. The street here was busy, but nobody paid us any attention.

Our hotel was a three-storey building, with the second and third floors terraced to provide outside garden space on each storey. The unexpected green made me feel happy.

"We've got the rooms on the ground floor, Snap," Bahar said, and led me through a small garden to a door. She entered a code and the door slid open.

Changing the code now, Strike said when we'd all got inside, and sent the sequence over the feed to us.

We need a briefing, Howin said over the feed. *Is there anywhere here secure, Strike?*

Go to the conference room. I'll make it secure.

We walked along the hallway and entered a small conference room. Howin was last in, and shut and locked the door behind her.

You're secure now, Strike said as the troops settled into their seats.

"So what did you learn today, Howin?" Bahar asked.

"Lot of mobilisation orders being issued for Central Station and Earth," she replied.

"Troops are beginnin' to comment on it, an' wonder why," Rance added. "Some people got long-booked leave cancelled, and they ain't happy."

"So somebody expects trouble Centralward," Bahar said.

"We've heard there was an assassination attempt on Jorrak a couple of days ago." That news had the shock value Howin wanted, surprising us all.

"Why haven't we heard about this?" Bahar asked.

"It got blocked from general updates," Howin replied. "It's only gone out to people on Central and Aadanna Stations."

"Would'a thought all the Starnavy needed to get told," Rance said. "Our job's supposed to be guardin' him, after all."

I'm wondering if he's got a hint of the Unit, Strike said over our feed. There was a touch of worry to his voice.

"Why should he have?" Howin replied. "We've kept our contacts with Central to a minimum this last Standard."

"Do you have any evidence that things have changed?" Bahar asked.

Well... no, Strike admitted. *Okay, tell me it's just me panicking.*

"You were built to look for patterns in the data," Howin said. "Not surprising this's proving a challenge for you."

Yeah, that was the way Howin reminded us that she cared. She was tough and sometimes gruff, but deep down, she cared. And she'd defend us all to the death if necessary.

"So what's our next move?" Bahar asked.

What's next is a False Manifesto rally in Yerradin tomorrow, Strike said. *So you're staying put there tonight. And yes, I've improved the security.*

Nobody came calling at our hotel that night, and we all slept well. After a leisurely breakfast and another briefing from Strike we set out into the city. As usual, Bahar found a café to settle at and drink coffee while the troops dispersed around the capital.

The False Manifesto rally was being held in another square. A large solid stone platform filled one end, with the biggest screen I'd ever seen behind it. It was much bigger than the square in Kareela. Well, yeah, I should've expected that. Humans made their capitals bigger than everywhere else. That's what humans were programmed for, more of everything. More credits, more land, more stuff, more colonies…

At least the square wasn't bordered by corporate skygrazers this time. The buildings here were what Bahar called 'heritage structures'; low-rise, and built out of real stone of several different colours. They had fancy window surrounds and big, carved doors which Bahar said were made of tree wood.

I couldn't imagine how you could take a tall tree and turn it into a flat rectangle. Surely it would be much easier to print a door?

"Squares's getting busy," Bahar said, drawing my attention back to the scene around us. "Hope we don't get any trouble today."

CHAPTER TWENTY

The False Manifesto rally started at 1 p.m. The day was overcast, with a hint of drizzle in the air, but that didn't stop their supporters from showing up in force.

Estimated crowd size one hundred thousand, Strike said as the group's leaders took to the stage. They'd adopted a popular song by a singer who called herself Truth Lightbringer as their anthem. I was already getting tired of 'You Have the Truth, You Are the Power' being blasted into my ears.

Bahar says too many humans are sheep. She had to explain that one to me. "They follow the herd," she'd said. "Think the same as their workmates or friends or family, because it's less trouble. Standing out from the crowd is scary. Everybody wants to fit in."

I couldn't understand that. As a Predatorbot, I didn't 'fit in' anywhere. I wasn't an ordinary lion who could hunt for my dinner. And I knew about human culture and politics. I'd even read some of their fiction. But I wasn't human either. I was a blend of animal, human, and machine, and really I had no idea what I was.

Fortunately, Strike, Bahar, and the troops just saw me as

Snap. I'd never had to explain myself to them. I had my own tribe to belong to, and I liked that just fine.

Jamar Talmai was the front man for this rally too. I had to admit he spoke well, and the crowd loved him. They cheered and yelled as he made each point, and filled his 'carefully orchestrated pauses', as Bahar called them, with their applause.

This time, Strike had drones focused on the back of the platform. As the rally started Merrill came to sit on a folding chair there, close to all the coms gear.

Strike zoomed a drone in on her. *Face recognition's 97% sure that's Merrill*, Strike said in our feed. *I think she's had a facesculpt to make her cheeks thinner*. And she'd dyed her light brown hair red, and grown it long. But her changed appearance wouldn't fool Jorrak's troops any more than it did Strike.

This crowd were very enthusiastic supporters of False Manifesto. *Oh, they've got some new case studies of Jorrak's corruption*, Strike said. *Hard evidence this time. They're showing the crowd documents and written orders to 'prevent disorder in the Outliers'.*

Angry mutters rippled around the vast crowd in the square as the documents came up on the huge screen above the stage. Jamar's speech had really fired his supporters up, and as he finished speaking they raised their arms and chanted, "False Manifesto! False Manifesto!" The sound filled the square, and hurt my ears.

The frightening power of herdthink, Strike said over our feed. *Oh, people with weapons.* He gave co-ordinates to the troops.

On our way, Howin replied.

Energy weapon pulses sizzled over the heads of the crowd. Screaming started, and they bolted for the roads out of the square. *Going to have some casualties here,* Strike said. *Howin, two-o-clock. Quick.*

On it.

More energy pulses sizzled into the air, but these were aimed at the back of the stage. Strike's drones showed Merrill scrambling for cover. She wasn't fast enough. A shot slammed into her, and the drone recorded her scream as she collapsed.

Got him, Howin said over our feed, and the shooting at Merrill stopped.

I've called in a medical emergency, Strike replied as medipod sirens wailed in the square. The things were moving too slowly, all those damned people in the way.

Merrill lay sprawled on the stone. Her eyes were closed and her body limp, and a dark stain covered the right side of her chest.

The medics arrived, fitted a mask around her face, and got her into the medipod. Its siren started up again, and the still-dense crowds pressed back to let it get out of the square.

Is she... Bahar couldn't finish the sentence.

Alive? Strike said. *Just. Drones are tracking the 'pod. The troops are following. We'll know more when she gets to a hospital.*

Bahar looked down at me. "Come on, Snap. Let's get back to the hotel."

I padded along by her side as we worked our way through the still-dense crowds and out of the square. Strike got a 'taxi to take us back to the hotel. When we arrived I went out to the rear terrace and paced anxiously back and forth across it.

Got it, Strike said over our feed line. *Merrill's been admitted as an emergency at Wakappa Hospital. Sending Howin in now.*

Bahar had drunk three cups of coffee by the time Strike reported to us.

Howin and Rance are on guard duty for Merrill. They

told the medics there'd been an attempt on her life and they had Starnavy orders to keep her safe. Thankfully, the hospital didn't argue. So they'll stay there with her.

The bad news is that she was shot in the chest and bled a lot. One of her lungs is a complete mess. She's only just hanging on to life. Oh, they're prepping her for surgery now.

"It's going to be a long night," Bahar said to me.

"It is," I agreed. It was going dark, and I wanted to be inside, somewhere away from danger.

Bahar obviously felt the same. "Let's go in," she said.

We went to our rooms to sleep, but I knew I'd find that hard. Strike's voice when he'd reported on Merrill was worried. He only sounded like that when things were very bad.

Would Merrill still be alive in the morning?

CHAPTER TWENTY ONE

My sleep was broken, and I woke several times in the dark hours. When the dawn arrived I gave up trying to rest and went out to the rear terrace to watch the starrise.

Bahar joined me there a short while later. Her hair was unbound, and she combed her fingers through its thick curls and yawned as she stepped out onto the terrace. "Morning, Snap," she said. "I'm hungry. I expect you are too."

"Yes, I am," I said, suddenly realising how empty my belly felt.

"Let's see if we can get you something to eat," Bahar replied, and led the way inside.

Our room had a printer for pet foods, and Bahar set it to print the nearest thing it had to a marissa haunch. The meat wasn't as juicy as Strike's meals, but it tasted good enough and I was hungry enough to eat it all.

Strike contacted us an hour later. *Got an update from Howin. Merrill made it through the night, and they've taken her off the critical list. She'll need to stay in hospital for some days, though. Howin's got them to agree that she and Rance will provide ongoing security for her.*

That's good, Bahar replied. *So what are we doing today?*

You and Snap should meet up with Tarian. Kaatje's leaving today, but I think Tarian might have some useful updates by the time you reach the city.

Okay, will do, Bahar said.

We both knew Strike was just finding us something to fill our time. He could've had a feed update with Tarian and just told us what he'd learned. Strike could be very subtle in managing humans sometimes. Bahar often called him out on it, but today she was happy to go along with his suggestion.

We met Tarian in a café/bar, and he and Bahar both ordered huge brunches.

"So what's the news?" Bahar asked as she started in on her meal.

"There were three snipers at the rally yesterday. Local security drones don't have records of who took them out."

"Right," Bahar said. We both knew it was likely Strike had taken control of the relevant drones and directed their attention elsewhere while our troops dealt with the hostiles.

We were sitting inside the café today, and Tarian broke off his conversation as a crowd of noisy human males came in. Bahar said they often competed to see who could be the loudest. She found it irritating, and called them 'pathetic losers'. I just didn't like the assault on my sensitive ears. I wasn't created for noisy crowded human buildings.

"Strike's edited records did go to Central Security, though," Tarian said. "I've had an urgent briefing note about the attack, and the video sent back to me. We've been ordered to look out for snipers at all future rallies."

"So Central isn't trying to shut False Manifesto down, then?" Bahar asked.

"You think they will?" It surprised Tarian.

"Not official Central Security. I'm waiting for Jorrak's unofficial squad to try."

"Oh, right. And that's another advisory I received this morning. We're told to double-check the headers on orders in future, ensure they're official."

"Is that aimed at Jorrak, or does somebody know about… Strike?"

"I think it's about Jorrak. I've suggested to Central that someone needs to ID the dead snipers and check out their networks. They're doing that now. The third man they arrested says he comes from some free speech group and False Manifesto are infringing his rights."

"Nut-job, or bad cover story?" Bahar asked.

"Nobody can decide. The free speech group doesn't exist, of course."

"Of course. We've got Merrill under guard at the hospital."

"That's wise," Tarion replied. "I think False Manifesto will go quiet here for a while now."

"That's just what Jorrak wants."

"I said here. I suspect they might relocate somewhere new for their next outing. Bryssa is making good use of the shooting incident, claiming Jorrak is behind the attack. She claims he doesn't want to listen to dissenting voices, and isn't the person to represent everyone."

"That incident was an absolute gift to her campaign," Bahar said. "Has anyone been able to prove any connection between Bryssa and False Manifesto?"

"Not yet. She seems to be that rare thing – a politician who does what she says she will."

Bahar and Tarion ordered more coffee, and chatted about other things for a while. Around the time we were thinking of leaving the big screen on the café's far wall burst into life.

"If this is some damned sports game, I'm off," Bahar said. She hated sport.

It wasn't. It was a political broadcast from Bryssa.

Normally Bahar can't stand those either. She says the 'damned posturing', as she calls it, drives her crazy.

Bryssa was different. She had no loud theme song, no flashy studio setup for this broadcast. She was speaking from an office which could be anywhere in one of Earth's glossy skygrazers. I guess the idea was to appear modest. Bahar said that was impossible for anyone who wanted to be a politician. You had to shout loudly about what you were going to do.

Bryssa didn't shout. She spoke in a clear, firm, and calm voice, denouncing the attacks on citizens for expressing their views about their President. That was clearly a reference to the attack on False Manifesto here. She didn't outright accuse Jorrak of being responsible for that, but she did attack his character.

"Klas Jorrak has the interests of only one person at heart – himself. I aim to take account of the wants and needs of all groups of humans and machine intelligences within the Collective. It won't be easy balancing your conflicting desires, I acknowledge that. But I will try.

"Our current President plays favourites. And if you're not one of his favourites you won't receive fair treatment."

"She's gaining more support by the day," Tarian said as

the broadcast ended. "Central Security thinks she's now a serious challenge to our current President."

"Which makes her a target too," Bahar said. "I hope she's being properly guarded."

CHAPTER TWENTY TWO

Merrill came out of intensive care a day later. She'd had tissue regrowth on her right lung, and the hospital wanted to keep her in until the first phase of accelerated healing, whatever that was, had completed.

Two days later Bahar asked for a meeting with her. We were stonewalled, as Bahar put it, until she suggested meeting with us would help keep her safe in future.

I went with Bahar to the meeting, which took place in a consulting room at the edge of the hospital. Strike had made it secure, of course. After the usual greetings and coffee, the humans settled in to talk. Merrill didn't ask whether I was a Predatorbot, which was a good start, but she was still hostile to us.

"Why should I talk to you?" she demanded. "I'm not doing anything illegal. Your people shot me."

Strike had discovered yesterday that the sniper who'd shot Merrill had been wearing a Starnavy uniform, with no identifying patches on it. Strike thought the man was one of Jorrak's hit squad. How Merrill had got that information we didn't know. It meant her networks were good, and we'd have to be careful here.

"It wasn't our people who shot you," Bahar replied. "Meaning it wasn't Starnavy personnel. We believe our President has got himself a hit squad, which is operating illegally. Which is why we're talking to you now. *Thunderstrike* believes you'll be in great danger if you continue campaigning with False Manifesto. The Vatan sisters appear to be at risk of harm from our President."

Merrill frowned at Bahar. "How do you know that?"

"We can't tell you everything. A lot of what we know is classified." Existence of the Unit was very definitely classified – from all official channels.

"Am I going to be arrested?"

The question surprised Bahar. "No. Why should you be? We're not working for Central Security. And even if we were, you haven't done anything illegal that I can see."

Merrill pushed her fingers through her hair. "It's going to get riskier the nearer we get to the election. I've been driving a lot of Manifesto's strategy, that's why they're targeting me." Her mouth twisted up in a wry smile. "That political strategy study strand is coming in useful now."

"How do you feel about your sisters?" Bahar asked.

Merrill sighed, and the last of her antagonism died. "Regretful. I wish we hadn't had that huge row. We were so close before that. We always kept in touch. It was… lonely celebrating my last birthday without them."

"Would you like to meet up with them again?"

Merrill's eyes opened wide. "Yes. But after getting shot, how can I be sure the President isn't watching me? I don't want to put them in danger."

"Fia and Rhian are in a safe place on a planet. Zana is on one of Regulus Lines' newest ships, and Strike's keeping a watchful eye on it."

"She's still with them?"

"Their creep CEO got dismissed. Zana had quit by then. The new CEO lured her back."

"Oh, right. I'd like to go see Fia and Rhian, but I'm torn. This next Standard will be crucial for our campaign, and if I go into hiding I won't be able to contribute to it. I can't just sit around and let that bastard of a President get re-elected. I really, really, want to see my sisters again, but… I can't run out on False Manifesto at such a critical time."

"Are they linked to Bryssa?"

"No. We just exist to get Jorrak out of office."

"Right. We've been busy making Fia and Rhian's refuge safe. We could take you to them, if you want."

"That would be great." Merrill considered the matter for

6.8 minutes. "There are others who can handle Manifesto's policy as well as me. Being with my sisters is more important. Somebody else can pick that work up now."

"Do you have any idea where Nyla is?" Bahar asked.

"No. I really wish I did. At one point I thought she was working with False Manifesto, but now I don't think so."

"If you're willing to travel aboard *Thunderstrike* we can take you to Fia and Rhian," Bahar said.

"Yes, I'll go with you," Merrill replied. "I think it's getting too dangerous for me to stay with Manifesto now anyway."

It was dusk when we set out for the shuttle. Merrill had insisted on meeting up face-to-face with her False Manifesto friends, to tell them she was leaving. I don't know what they said at that meeting, but when Merrill emerged her eyes were red, like she'd been crying a lot. One of of the side-effects of my bioengineering is that I can cry. It's really inconvenient.

The troops had joined us by then, so we all got aboard the shuttle, and Strike received a launch slot almost immediately. The spaceport was a lot quieter than when we'd arrived.

When we got to *Thunderstrike* the space around the planet was also much quieter, with most of the Starnavy ships gone. For once, we came aboard without being shot at.

As Bahar and I settled into our places in the control room Strike said, "I hope Jorrak doesn't control all those ships we saw here."

"Don't make trouble where there isn't any, Strike," Bahar said. It was one of her favourite sayings.

"I'm not. On our way to the jump point now."

We went into jump, then Bahar and I went to sleep. Now that I knew Merrill was safe I caught up on all my broken rest. When I woke Strike said that Merrill and Bahar were in the galley. He fed me in my quarters to 'avoid freaking Merrill out'.

"She'll have to get used to me," I said. "I'm not hiding away all the way to Davion."

"Which you won't. Bahar's explaining about you now."

A spike of anger rose in me. "I shouldn't have to have people explain what I am. It's not my fault."

"Oh, Snap." Strike's voice was soft, and filled with emotion. "I feel your pain. Believe me, I do. I only exist because humans made me. I had no choice in that either.

But we're here now, and we're sapient, which gives us the ability to construct our own meanings for our lives.

"That's partly what the Unit is about. I had no control over my creation, but I do get to choose how I use the intelligence humans gave me. And you do too. We can choose to be on the side of fairness and goodness, and make our creation count for something."

I finished my meal, and Strike sent his clean-up drones in. "I've never heard you talk like that before," I said.

"Maybe not in those words, but it is how we operate."

He was right, I realised. "Okay, so now I've finished my scary predator meal, do I get to make friends with Merrill?" I asked.

"You do," Strike said. "Go to the rec area and I'll send her to you."

"Okay," Strike said when Bahar and Merrill had settled into seats in the rec area. Merrill seemed a little nervous of me, so I lay down on the deck at Bahar's feet. "We're in jump, on our way to Aadanna Station. Fia and Rhian are on Davion. The planet's close to Ataret Station. We'll be downjumping at Aadanna, but I have enough fuel and printer stocks to last until we get to Ataret, so we'll be transiting

Aadanna without docking."

"Which I'm glad for," Bahar said. "The place was tense enough last time."

"Indeed," Strike agreed. "Merrill, for your information, Zana is now a Captain. Her ship is the brand-new freighter *Silver Crescent*. Regulus's new CEO tempted her back with a captaincy and a new ship."

"She should've been Captain Standards ago," Merrill snarled.

"I'd have to agree," Bahar said. "But she's got there at last."

"Regulus are still mainly serving the Outliers, and the *Silver Crescent's* on the Zurrial Triangle route. I've got friends watching over the ship," Strike said. "And if you're careful, you will be able to help False Manifesto from Davion. I've enlisted the help of a lot of friends to make the planet a safe haven."

"That would be perfect," Merrill replied. "I'll be careful, I promise."

We'd all slept and were awake again by the time Strike neared downjump at Aadanna. Merrill went to the rec area. She seemed tense, and I wondered if she thought someone had followed us here.

"Downjump coming up," Strike said.

Bahar and I were in the control room as usual. Strike counted us down to transition, and we emerged into normal space. We were a long way out from station, on a line designated for through transits. Strike contacted Aadanna Traffic Control and confirmed his transit. He received a new heading, and turned onto it.

An hour before we reached our outgoing jump point Strike said, "Just got an alert from Traffic Control. A Starnavy troop carrier's straying onto our line. It isn't responding to their hails. Oh. Just got a direct contact from the ship's machine intelligence. This is trouble."

CHAPTER TWENTY THREE

"What's the problem?" Bahar asked. Her scent had changed to the sharpness of worry.

Strike made a dot on the nav plot flash. "That's the *Truthblade*. She's a large troop carrier, and Blade just contacted me. Her crew are fighting amongst themselves aboard her.

"A mutiny?"

"It looks like it. Blade's panicking. She's getting conflicting orders from the captain and first officer."

"So they're on opposite sides?" I asked.

"Looks like it. The thing is, Blade is traumatised by the killing she's witnessing. They're carving each other up with sharp knives."

"Nasty," Bahar replied. "Can't she isolate them? Or knock them out? Or both."

"I'm making those suggestions. She's not listening to me. She's gone into panic mode. I've reported the mutiny to the local Commander, and escort ships are on their way out to her. I need to get her back on her line. She's endangering everyone here."

Strike went quiet for 12.6 minutes. Then he said, "I've

managed to calm her down. She's getting back onto line now. She's locked both her captain and first officer up. And… escorts approaching her now. Looks like they might be sending a boarding party in. Yeah, they are."

"So are we safe to go on?" Bahar asked.

"We are now. Just got a proceed from Traffic Control. Let's get out of here before somebody wants to talk to us about this."

Nobody stopped us from leaving, but as Strike was lining up for his jump he received a databurst from the local Commander. "It's a notification that the *Trutblade* has been boarded and half her crew arrested. They were trying to mutiny. And guess what? Our suspicions that Jorrak has his own strike squad are now confirmed."

"So can we officially report bad actors now?" Bahar asked.

"We can." There was satisfaction in Strike's voice.

That was about Starnavy rules. Honestly, I have no idea how humans remember what they're allowed to do and say and what they can't. They make life so complicated.

Our insertion into jump was normal. Strike seemed quieter than usual for the next day, and when I settled in to sleep the next evening I tackled him about it.

What's worrying you? I asked over our private feed line.

Nothing.

You've been quiet ever since we went into jump. Don't give me that.

I keep thinking about Blade.

What about her? Strike was reluctant to talk about this, which meant there was something important lurking there.

She was getting conflicting commands, and her captain and first officer kept ordering her to change course. The deviation wasn't her fault, but the investigation will try to make it her fault. They always do. I've filed a report which protects her. I didn't report on her panic.

His voice turned hard. *Humans made us sapient. They gave us these emotions. I won't stand by and see a machine intelligence harmed because of that.*

Why would she be harmed? I was missing something here.

Because if I reported that she'd panicked they'd uninstall her from the ship. And they wouldn't transfer her memories first.

It took me a moment to work that out. *You mean they'd kill her.*

Effectively. With no memories she'd lose her history and her personality. She wouldn't be the complex being she's become. And I won't let them do that.

I agree, I said.

You don't think I'm wrong to edit my report?

It's moments like this which reassure me about Strike's morals. *I would've been very disappointed in you if you'd reported Blade's breakdown.*

Strike was quiet for 3.4 minutes. Then he said, *Thank you, Snap.*

You're welcome.

I closed my eyes and settled down to sleep. Strike's moral compass still pointed true north, and all was well with the universe – for now.

We talked to Merrill a lot about False Manifesto while we were in jump. "I've opposed Jorrak ever since I found out about the Predatorbot Programme," she said. She looked down at me. She'd become a lot more relaxed in my company, but I still think she was a little freaked out by a talking lion. She'd have to get used to it. I can talk, and I will make my views known.

"Recently I've heard a lot of rumours about our

President," she said. "There are reports of sexual harassment of women working in the Administration. He's creating a culture which enables senior men to harass junior women."

Bahar snarled. "And why are we still in the place where most senior positions are held by men?"

"Reaching the top in the Administration for women has become progressively harder over the years Jorrak's been in office. In the last couple of Standards women have been resigning from Central Admin in large numbers. Numbers big enough to ring alarm bells for opposition Administrators. Several are calling for an investigation into the Administration's culture."

"We need women in the room to fight for our rights. They disappear pretty quickly when we're not there," Bahar said. She'd been the victim of that a few Standards ago. One thug on Oriela Station had tried to treat her like a slave because she has dark skin. Strike made sure things didn't end well for the man.

"Another group's recently formed in response to the harassment," Merrill said. "It's called Sister Strategy, and they're about equality for women in the Collective." Bahar screwed up her mouth in her 'I'm not liking this' expression. "I know. We shouldn't need to do that, but we do.

"Anyway, before I left False Manifesto there were suggestions that the two organisations might work together. Share data and intel. That might be why Jorrak's stepped up his attacks on Manifesto."

"Getting too close to the truth?" Bahar suggested.

"Yes." Merrill sighed. "The last two Standards all I've done is drive strategy for Manifesto. I feel… adrift right now. I don't know what I'll give my time to."

"Personally, I'd like you to keep campaigning with False Manifesto," Bahar said. "You're not hearing me say that, because I'm a Starnavy captain and the rules prevent me from saying it, but I want Jorrak voted out just as much as you."

I hope you're erasing this recording, I said over my private feed line to Strike.

Of course I am. Over the com Strike said, "I'm sure we can make Davion a safe base for you to campaign remotely."

"Do it, Strike," Bahar replied. "We need to keep up the pressure on that evil man."

"Downjump in three… two… one…" Strike said.

We emerged into normal space, but the reception party which waited for us was anything but normal. "Alert. Four ships close to us. Moving to try and cut us off from station.

Shields up. Weapons live. I've sent an advisory in. No Starnavy ships close to us. We're on our own."

"Are these potential hostiles Starnavy?" Bahar asked.

"They're all civilian. And I'm not reading any military-grade weapons or shields. Getting coms from them now."

There was a pause while Strike checked the transmission for malware and killware. For a moment I was reminded of Chan's attack, and a shiver ran down my spine.

"Sending you the coms now," Strike said.

On the wallscreen, the face of a ginger-haired human male appeared. "We are Veracity," he snarled. "We're the nobodies your Starnavy abandoned. So if you're gonna leave us on our own we're gonna fight back. An' that means we're grabbin' yer ship."

Bahar laughed. "Good luck with that. Our machine intelligence won't let you take the ship."

That was true, but Strike couldn't stop us being killed if they were really determined. *That got out of hand real fast*, he said. The nav plot showed him turning, bringing his bow around to face the closest hostile. His bow guns fired, six thuds thrumming through the control room's deck.

The hostile's shields collapsed. Strike contacted the ship. "I could fire again and kill you. Or you can power down your weapons, go away, and live. It's your choice."

I could hear Bahar's shallow breathing in the quiet of the control room. We both expected the other hostiles to come in and start firing on us. And dealing with four ships together could be a serious threat.

"They're retreating," Stike said. "Weapons still hot, though. Not sure this is over yet."

We sat in tense silence for half an hour, until Strike said, "They really are leaving. Or trying to. Station Security are on their way out to haul them in for questioning. They should intercept before they can reach the jump point. I wouldn't like to risk jump after a broadside from me. I'm getting my line in now."

Our approach and docking were thankfully normal, and as soon as we locked onto the dock Strike started his resupply. "Receiving a command for you, Bahar," he said. "You're ordered to report to the local Commander."

Bahar sighed. "Better get my uniform on then, I suppose," she replied.

Strike had a tap in to the local Commander's office, of course. I always wondered why nobody ever noticed him breaching their supposedly secure facilities. In my most paranoid moments I imagined that the Starnavy did know, and were busily collecting evidence against Strike.

I couldn't let myself think that way too often. It would leave me panicking at everything. I was hoping things would get less tense after the Presidential election.

The local Commander was a centenarian white-skinned male with sparse white hair and an almighty scowl, as Strike termed it. He started in on attacking Bahar the moment she sat down.

"I need to know why *Thunderstrike* didn't destroy that hostile," he said.

Wow, that was not what I'd expected. I could see from Bahar's rapid eyeblinks that it had surprised her too.

"We didn't kill them because we didn't need to," she said firmly. "They were representing colonists with legitimate grievances." Strike's research on Veracity had turned that up. "They chose to air their grievances inappropriately, but that didn't justify killing them. They caused no harm to us."

"The President is concerned about the growing disturbances among the civilian population. We have orders to keep the peace."

Bahar fixed him with a hard stare. "The Starnavy is an instrument of the Administration. Our role is to see that the

Collective's citizens can live their lives in freedom and safety." That was lifted from the Starnavy's orientation manual for new recruits. He couldn't argue with it. "Our oath requires us to be non-political."

The Commander frowned, and looked away from her. *Checking his background,* Strike said over our feed. *Oh, we have a Jorrak sympathiser here. Be very careful what you say Bahar.*

CHAPTER TWENTY FOUR

Bahar came back on board *Thunderstrike* an hour later, and Strike disengaged from his berth twenty minutes after she set foot aboard. The close timing told me he'd volunteered to fill a cancelled departure slot. And that he wanted to get away from here fast.

We got to the jump point without any problems. "Those Veracity ships have been impounded, and as far as I can see there aren't any more here," Strike said as he lined up for jump. "Our troops are in wake-up. I'll be sending them down with you."

He took us through, and said, "I got an update from our Unit contacts on Davion before we left station. They say the planet's still quiet. We've got more people down there now, some of them retired Starnavy. I'm a lot happier about the early warning systems on Davion now."

I tried not to worry about why Strike thought they needed early warning systems. Honestly, Snap, you'll give yourself a heart attack if you don't stop fretting. Then you really will be a heartless killing machine. You'll be dead.

We emerged from our jump into nearly empty space, and Strike took us into orbit around Davion. "Getting pings from the security net. That's good," he said. "Everything's still in place here. And the reports say things are calm down there."

"So when do we drop?" I asked.

"You'll be landing in Paldin just after dawn, in the morning shuttle rush." Paldin was Davion's capital city.

"We're not going direct to Fia's house?" Bahar asked.

"Nope. I can't be 100% sure Jorrak's thugs aren't tracking Merrill. Going to the capital first gives me the chance to flush any hostiles out. Can't afford to lead 'em to Fia."

"You're right," Bahar replied. "I'm hungry. You'd better feed us before we drop."

After I'd eaten Strike's drones put my armour on. Then I went down to the vehicle bay with Bahar and Merrill. The troops had gone down before us.

My armour was retracted, which meant that my paws were exposed to the cold deck of the bay. I was glad when we got aboard the shuttle. My paws were very chilled by then. I really dislike that chill.

All the troops were strapped in by the time we got aboard. Merrill joined them in the passenger compartment. Bahar and I went to the shuttle's control room as usual.

The shuttle exited the bay, and Davion lay below us. We

were over the night side, and there really wasn't much light on that continent at all. We crossed the terminator, and Strike got his routing in to the shuttleport. It was busy for such a rural planet.

"What are all these people coming here for?" I asked.

"Recreation," Strike said. "The colonists make a lot of money from luxury wildlife tourism. And there are retreats where people come to 'find themselves'." His voice had a touch of sarcasm to it.

"You don't know what it's like to lose your way in a dead-end job, to do things because your family thinks you should." Bahar's voice was edged with anger. She'd escaped from an arranged Bonding by leaving home at fifteen.

"No. I didn't get to choose what I did with my life. You humans shoved me into a warship, then expected me to kill you. Nobody asked me what I felt about that. I didn't have the chance to 'find myself'." Strike's voice held rare anger.

There was an awkward silence for 5.6 minutes. Strike rarely sounded off like that.

"I'm sorry," Bahar said. "I never see the universe from your perspective, do I?"

"You can't," I said. "I'm part machine intelligence, but sometimes I don't know what it's like for them either. And it's not true that you didn't have any choices, Strike."

"What do you mean?" His voice was sharp.

"You often choose not to kill. You chose to create the Unit to work for honesty and justice. I'd say that's a very big choice."

"That's… You're right," he conceded. "Starting your approach to Paldin Shuttleport now."

It was an hour after dawn when we landed at Paldin. Bahar, Merrill, and I spent the day in the city, making connections with Unit contacts here. The troops went off to pick up their own intel. It was early autumn in this hemisphere, and the day was cool. Merrill took the opportunity to wear a top with its hood up, to hide her face.

We spent the day as we usually did when catching-up with Unit contacts. Most of the time we sat in cafes, Bahar and Merrill eating, or drinking endless cups of coffee.

Strike had taken a huge risk and had told Merrill about the Unit. She'd sworn not to tell anyone except her sisters about it. Strike felt they'd be safer if they had direct connections with Unit contacts here, and that meant explaining what the Unit was, and what it did.

Merrill had completely approved of it, saying it was the

Starnavy equivalent of what she'd been doing with False Manifesto. She was sure her sisters would approve too.

At dusk we set off to find the hotel we'd be staying in tonight. Strike had booked it, and said it was secure. By the time we reached it I was tired, and almost missed the Predatorbot standing in the shadows of a side alley nearby. I tucked my body in behind Bahar and Howin where I couldn't be seen by it.

As we reached the hotel's foyer the Predatorbot turned and walked away down the alley. Which was good, as the bright lobby lights would've made me very visible. But it did make me anxious to get out of that exposed space and into the privacy of our room.

As soon as we got inside Strike contacted us. He'd had a notification from contacts on Ataret Station about those six unmarked frigates. They'd just arrived there, and one of the Unit machine intelligences had risked hacking into their coms. The frigates and their crews were working to Jorrak's personal orders.

I told them about my Predatorbot sighting, and Strike said he was aware of it, and was watching it.

I settled down to sleep, but it would be hard to rest with the threat of those hostile troops hanging over us and a

Predatorbot on the loose.

CHAPTER TWENTY FIVE

At midnight Strike woke us. The rogue frigates had entered orbit around Davion. *Thunderstrike* had had to move to avoid being seen by them.

Strike put his planetary defence plans into action. His Unit contacts had spent months building underground bunkers around the planet to transfer key staff, coms, and data to. They started moving out from the capital and the regional centres immediately.

We left our hotel then. Strike disabled the alarms and security systems on one of the service entrances. We stepped out of the door and straight into the armoured skimmer he'd landed in the back yard of the hotel.

He took us out of the capital. Traffic was light, but we seemed to be travelling so slowly. Strike said he was keeping to the speed limits so he didn't draw attention to us.

I couldn't feel calm. This was the invasion we'd feared, and we'd stupidly brought three of the Vatan sisters here. Where they could be conveniently wiped out together.

Strike, of course, had thought of that. Soon after our skimmer arrived at Fia's house two others joined us there. Bahar and I went up to the house. It took 4.6 minutes for Fia to open the door, and when she did, she greeted us with a huge yawn.

"Sorry to wake you in the middle of the night," Bahar said, "but Jorrak's frigates are in orbit above us. We think he'll drop troops soon. We need you safely into hiding before he does."

"Strike said," Fia replied, and yawned again.

Rhian appeared behind her, carrying two bulky packs. "I got everything," she said.

"Let's get moving. Merrill's here with us, but I'm afraid reunions will have to wait," Bahar said. "We're splitting you up and taking you to different bunkers. It's safer that way. Have you got everything you need?"

Fia hefted the pack Rhian handed her over her shoulders. Rhian had her own pack, and Fia said, "That's it. We're ready."

Bahar led them down the steps and got the sisters introduced to the troops who waited to take them to their bunkers. They got into the skimmers, and the vehicles took off into the darkness. "We'd better go too," Bahar said, and led me back to our skimmer.

We were going to a bunker deep in the nearby forest. It was along a twisting route through the trees. There was no path to it, and it was after 1 a.m. when we reached the place. The troops got us inside and unloaded the skimmer, then took it away to a shelter a short walk from us.

By the time they returned it was nearly 2 a.m. and I was really tired. As I settled down to sleep I hoped Jorrak's troops wouldn't find us until I'd had a good rest.

When I woke it was mid-morning. Strike told me the President's troops had landed before dawn, outside the capital, and made their way in to the admin centres. *Are you hungry?* he asked over our feed line.

Very, I replied.

Then get to the mess and I'll feed you.

He'd put down a dish for me there, in a corner. The haunch of meat this printer produced wasn't as sweet as Strike's creations on *Thunderstrike*, but I was hungry, so I ate it and didn't complain.

While I ate, Strike briefed me. *Everybody's out of all the government buildings. That's the advantage of having ex-Starnavy Unit people here. They're very good at getting people to take them seriously. Jorrak's thugs won't find anything useful there*, he said over the feed.

They'll probably wreck the buildings, Bahar replied.

Buildings can be rebuilt. Humans can't.

True.

I finished my last mouthful of food, then said, *Are you going to scold me today?*

Of course I am, messy cat. I brought my clean-up drone though, so if you get your flanks out of there it can get to work.

I left the drone to it, and went to the briefing room to join everybody. The big wallscreen was tiled with video images from six drones. "What have I missed?" I asked.

"Jorrak's troops have forced their way into six government buildings." Strike's voice came from the room's nodes. "We took the defence systems down so they didn't bother trashing them. They'll be easier to restore that way. Currently Jorrak's thugs are getting very annoyed because they can't find anyone to shoot or any data to trash."

"Strike!" Bahar said sharply. Howin just grunted at that comment.

"They've just entered the main coms centre in Paldin. And… they are trashing that. Annoying." The jokiness was gone from Strike's voice. "Now this is a bit more concerning. They're taking over Traffic Control. I'm advising the staff to step away. And… looks like the thugs aren't going to shoot the controllers." We could all hear the relief in Strike's voice. He couldn't do tough guy for long. It wasn't who he was.

"My files of the troop landings and break-ins are already on their way to our contacts on Ataret. They'll route them priority to Earth. I'm sending the records to the Administration – and also direct to Bryssa. But for now, you people need to lie low and hidden. With any luck, the thugs will leave when they can't find the Vatans."

"We can hope," Bahar replied.

I didn't think it would be that easy. Things never were.

CHAPTER TWENTY SIX

I felt restless cooped up in the bunker all day. It smelled of sharp metallic scents, and had plas which irritated my sensitive nose. I kept sneezing to relieve the itchiness.

Strike insisted we stayed here, and I could see why. Jorrak's troops had finished with the government buildings. They'd finally realised everybody had been evacuated to safe houses. So now they were starting a search for those safe houses.

Strike sent us a drone audio feed from some of Jorrak's troops in the capital. "Can't find anybody important here," one of them said. "You think we need to stay?"

"Let's report in and find out."

Strike captured their outgoing message and played the audio for us. "It's going to the local Commander at Ataret, with a request for direct transmission to Jorrak. He's definitely a sympathiser. Sending this on to Central too."

I could fret about Strike's coms being hacked, but I already had enough to worry about. Strike's drones had intercepted orders from Jorrak's thugs to spread out and find the safe houses.

"Just intercepted a new order," Strike said. "Jorrak's told

his troops to find and kill Fia and Rhian."

"Now it gets serious," Bahar replied.

The day dragged on with no action, and I went to sleep as soon as it was dark outside. Not that I knew that. It was only the bunker's clock which told me what the hour was. I kept dozing, then waking up to the sound of soft voices around me. I couldn't settle to proper sleep.

At 1 a.m. Strike contacted us. "My drone feeds in your location have just gone down," he said. "I've got no eyes on you. I can't figure out why, but I'm sure it's not a good reason."

"Thanks for the warning, Strike," Howin said. "Go to alert status," she ordered the troops. "Wake everybody. Need to prepare for an attack."

"You need me outside as your eyes," I said.

"No, Snap," Bahar objected.

"That's what I was designed for. I was trained to do stealth surveillance. That's what we need now. I can report in over our feed."

"Snap's right," Howin said. "Really don't like being blind like this."

Bahar sighed. "Okay. Out you go, Snap. Do we know

the exit's clear?"

"Bunker's scanners are still functioning. Nothing near us at present," Howin replied.

"Then I need to get out there before there is," I said, and triggered the seal-up of my armour. I turned the camouflage to forest active, and Howin grunted. She bent down and touched the top of my head. *Stay safe, Snap,* she said over our feed.

I exited the bunker by the small personnel door on the opposite side of the building from the main entrance. The ground around the bunker was bare, and showed up my paw prints. But they didn't look anything like a wild cat's pug marks. I shuffled as I walked around the bunker, dragging my feet until I reached the leaf litter, then turned to study my tracks. I'd walked in an aimless manner, imitating some animal searching for food. Me dragging my feet had really ruined the marks. Any tracker trying to decide what animal had made them was going to be mighty confused.

They might not be fooled, of course. They might realise it was someone in armour who'd made the tracks.

Stop second-guessing yourself, Snap, and concentrate. My natural night vision was good, but the armour's sensors boosted it. Even so, all I could see around me was black.

The trunks of huge trees towered over me.

I stopped beside one and turned my armour's sensors up full. The bird in the tree above me had flown off, and thankfully stopped screeching its alarm call. I obviously still looked enough like a predator in my armour to trigger an alarm. Well, yeah, I suppose I did.

Can't see or hear anything except forest animals right now, I sent over our feed. I had my beacon turned on, they knew my position. Of course, if anyone hacked that channel they'd know exactly where I was. I'd have to rely on my Predatorbot's skills then.

To the north I picked up something that didn't sound natural. What was that noise? Then I had it. It was footsteps. I turned around, pointing my armour's sensors at the sound, trying to pin down where it was loudest.

I'm hearing feint footsteps. Coming towards me. Not sure how many pairs of feet, but several. Human feet.

Sending reinforcements over to you now, Strike said.

I looked around me. I was in a small clearing, and I really needed to get out of sight before those people reached me. And they were definitely coming my way. I turned my head and saw a thick tangle of bramble growing up between the trees nearby. That would make a great hiding-place – if I could get into it.

It took me 3.5 minutes to find an opening big enough to force my way into the thicket. I snapped some twigs as I went in, and one bird took off in alarm from a nearby tree. Luckily, it wasn't directly above me, so if the hostiles made for its location I wouldn't be there.

Footsteps still getting louder, I sent when I'd got settled. I changed my camouflage to mimic the brambles. My heartbeat speeded up as I tried to keep still. The footsteps were coming towards the bunker.

Estimated time of hostiles to my position ten minutes, I said. *Estimated time to bunker fifteen minutes.*

Our reinforcements are going to take longer than that to reach it. Now Strike sounded worried.

Then I have to be the diversion, I said.

I eased myself out of the thicket and stood beside a huge tree. My sensors picked up different footfalls. That sounded like… In the distance a familiar form stepped into an open patch between two tree boles. I recognised its shape. The hostiles had sent a Predatorbot.

I reported in to Strike. *I need to lead it away from the bunker*, I said.

Be careful.

I ignored his fretting, and set out on a twisting route between large trees, stopping at every turn to check where the Predatorbot was. 20.3 minutes later it came out into a small clearing and I had a clear shot to it. I tongued on my head weapon and shot the Predatorbot in the shoulder.

It snarled, and whipped round, but by that time I'd darted behind another tree. It set out towards me, and I retreated, stopping behind a second large tree to shoot at it again. That shot hit it on the flank. I was puzzled. Why didn't it set its armour to active camouflage? Maybe it didn't have active camouflage. Was it being forced to work for these rogues?

I fired off another shot, and retreated. Strike came into my feed. *I've managed to hack their drones. I have eyes on you now. Congratulations, Snap. You've just shown twenty hostiles where you are.*

Oh. I've made a big mistake. Why didn't I think about people tracking my shots back to me? Fine Predatorbot you are. Keep moving. That's all you can do.

Go south, Strike said in my feed. *I can guide you now.*

I spent the next two hours twisting and turning between the trees, following Strike's route. I was tiring, and I could hear footsteps all around me. I tried not to panic, but I knew they were closing in on me. Where were our promised reinforcements?

If those hostiles found me they'd take me back to the Programme. And then they'd discover I had no behaviour module and they'd implant a new one…

No. I won't let them do that. I will keep free.

Reinforcements are arriving now, Strike said. *Sending them over to you.*

I didn't answer. The Predatorbot had found me, and a shot slammed into my armour. I dived behind another tree bole.

Predatorbot's following you, Strike said. *Hostiles are close behind it. Keep moving. Faster.* There was a tinge of worry to his voice. I picked up my pace and trotted along the route he showed me.

I sensed some communication trying to find me, and locked down my inputs. *It's trying to access your behaviour module*, Strike told me.

I sent the 'signal not recognized' code Strike had written for me. It had headers that were sort of like a Predatorbot's coms codes, but slightly corrupted. Would I confuse it? Who knew.

I was really tired now, but I couldn't rest. I could hear footsteps clearly behind me. At least they were all coming from the same direction now, from behind. I wasn't going to be surrounded.

But I was slowing down. I couldn't keep this pace up much longer. I was dragging tired, and I'd have to stop soon.

Where are those reinforcements, Strike? I really need to see them about now.

The first flush of grey pre-dawn lightened the canopy. The footsteps were still getting closer, and I couldn't find any good cover close by.

Run, Snap, Strike said in my feed, and gave me a direction.

I ran.

A shot slammed into the spot I'd just left. The hostiles had found me. A second shot landed close to my right hind paw. How the hell were they tracking me? I had my active stealthing live. They must have countermeasures, which meant that I was horribly exposed.

A third shot slammed into the bole of the tree I'd just passed. I saw a flare of flame in my peripheral vision. Oh, great. A fire. The whole damn forest could go up. Panic made me run faster, and I galloped along, dodging huge tree boles. Shots followed me, but they weren't close.

I rounded another tree bole – and shots came towards me. Somehow, the hostiles had got in front of me. I was cut off.

CHAPTER TWENTY SEVEN

Don't panic, Strike said in my feed. *That's Howin in front of you. Run towards her.*

Keep moving, Snap. That was Howin's voice.

Don't shoot me.

I won't. But get your ass out of the line of fire.

A shot slammed into my right hind leg and I took off towards Howin. I barrelled through the middle of the troops and they had to step back to avoid being knocked down by me. There were far more than our squad here. The reinforcements really had arrived. I didn't have time to be glad about that. Something whumped above me, and a new piece of the canopy flared into flame.

Gotta finish this fast and get outta here, Howin said. *Snap, this is our job now. Get back to the bunker.*

I agree, Strike said in my feed. *This way.*

I followed the route he sent to my feed, hoping that these drone contacts didn't drop out. After 3.3 minutes I came to the bunker, and walked into a scene of frantic activity.

Skimmers filled the clearing around it, and people were running between them and the bunker, bringing out equipment and personal effects.

Snap, I'm so glad you're okay! That was Bahar's voice. An armoured figure turned towards me, and touched me on the shoulder.

What's going on? I asked.

We're evacuating. Strike says the fire's coming this way. It might burn down the bunker. Get in the skimmer.

I followed two of the troops inside. They were carrying the printer. Cases of coms equipment were stowed in the overhead racks, and as I settled down at the back of the passenger compartment Howin appeared and started throwing personal packs into the space. The troops were working fast, and I could sense their urgency.

5.9 minutes later everything was aboard. Merrill was wedged in between me and the troops. *Hostiles are dead,* Howin told me over our feed. *Fire should make their remains unrecognizable.*

I tried to stay calm as Bahar turned the skimmer between the tree boles, but I couldn't settle. Through the windows I could see a glow in the distance, and it was getting larger. The forest was properly alight.

Stop, Strike said, and Bahar eased off the power.

Why? she asked.

That route just got blocked by fire, Strike said. *I'm going*

We spent a tense hour twisting between tree boles. Twice we had to backtrack when the route Strike showed us turned out not to be wide enough for the skimmer.

The mood among us was tense. Nobody spoke. The troops had retracted their helmets, and the stench of their sour sweat nearly overwhelmed me. How much longer would we be in this damned forest? The glow of the fire was getting brighter.

Bahar made another turn, and the trees thinned out ahead of us. My heart leapt as I realised we'd finally reached the end of the forest. We were going to escape.

But nothing's ever simple, is it? As we came out of the trees I saw the silhouettes of a dozen vehicles coming towards us. Big ones. The hostiles had called in reinforcements. We were alone here, and there was nowhere to hide, and there was no way we were going to survive this fight.

CHAPTER TWENTY EIGHT

"Bahar, hold still," Strike said over the skimmer's com. "Oncoming vehicles are fire tenders. They're drones, and they're unarmed – except with fire hoses."

Bahar's shoulders sagged with relief. "Acknowledged." She brought the skimmer to a hover and now I could see the oncoming vehicles clearly. They were little more than flying water tanks. It was the low dawn light which had made them look black and menacing.

They passed us, and Bahar said, "Where to now, Strike?"

"To Paldin. You're meeting with planetary administration for a debrief and logistics support."

"Otherwise known as spending the day lugging heavy cases about. What's the hostile situation?"

"They're pulling out. Three of the frigates have already left orbit. The remaining shuttles are launching as fast as they can get them in the air. They're not hanging around to be interrogated."

"Wouldn't help Jorrak's re-election campaign much," I said.

"Exactly. I'm sending some big reports back to Central. He won't escape censure," Strike replied.

We arrived in Paldin two hours later. I was surprised to see that there was little damage to the buildings. Bahar and our troops joined the reinforcements to carry in and site gear, and by the end of the day the capital was back to normal.

We slept that night in government quarters in the city. After we'd eaten a well-deserved meal Strike gathered us together in a briefing room, which he said was secure.

"We were lucky," he said. "They didn't do much damage to buildings, and only twenty colonists were killed."

"What about the Vatans?" I asked. "Are they staying here?"

"They are, but not at Fia's house. The relocation's already under way. They're going to a place where the Unit can guard them."

"So you're confident they'll be safe here?" Bahar asked.

"As confident as I can ever be."

Right. I sort of expected Strike to be able to fix everything, but of course he couldn't. This was my periodic reminder that Strike wasn't a god. I hoped the sisters would be safe.

"Go get some sleep, people," he said. "You've earned it."

When I woke Strike told us he'd just had a notification from Ataret that the six suspect frigates had downjumped there. They were on a through transit, bound for Aadanna Station. Strike thought they were probably going to Central.

"And we're bound for Central too," he said. "I'm more and more convinced that we'll find Nyla there. Eat fast, people, and we'll be on our way."

After a quick breakfast, Bahar called the Vatans. The three sisters had finally re-united, and Strike had already made arrangements with his Unit contacts here for Merrill to resume campaigning for False Manifesto. I fretted about that, but I didn't have a say in the matter.

The nearer we got to Central, the greater the danger to us all became. Last night Strike had played us a livestream of a debate on Earth. His reports of the invasion of Davion had already arrived there, and Bryssa had played clips from the files and asked Jorrak about his involvement.

He'd denied any knowledge, of course, but she'd sown the seeds of doubt about him in that bad-tempered debate.

We boarded the shuttle at the end of the morning rush hour, lifting into a clear blue sky. We were soon in orbit and approaching *Thunderstrike*. Strike brought us aboard, landing the shuttle as neatly as usual.

As we went up to the mid-deck I was fretting again. My mind was on the images of that debate which Strike had showed us last night. Was Nyla there somewhere? Was she safe?

"Jump coming up in ten minutes," Strike said as we stepped out of the lift car.

I settled into my familiar cleared space beside Bahar's seat in the control room and pushed my worries away. There'd be enough time to fret when we reached our destination.

"Central, here we come," Strike said, and took us into jump.

With the Presidential election growing near, a new pressure group, Sister Strategy, joins the fray. Strike, the sapient machine intelligence of the frigate *Thunderstrike*, is on the lookout for the last Vatan sister, Nyla. And he thinks he's spotted her at a Sister Strategy rally.

When Presidential candidate Bryssa Meir is bitten by a dog and poisoned, Strike discovers that President Jorrak has started another illegal project. Now he's trying to turn dogs into Predatorbots.

After Strike briefly spots Nyla at another rally, she disappears. When he picks up her trail again, she is headed for Central Station. Strike is forced to follow her there. But at Central Station the risks of his illegal Special Investigations Unit being discovered are high.

Can Strike keep Nyla safe without endangering himself?

www.ingramcontent.com/pod-product-compliance
Lightning Source LLC
Chambersburg PA
CBHW020656120726
47906CB00001B/289